"Dato' Dr Shan is a master
demonstrates. His distinctiv
make for a most pleasurable, rewarding and stimulating ...

—**HRH Sultan Nazrin Shah**

"Dr M. Shanmughalingam allowed me to read his work, which proved invaluable to my understanding of the Tamils. I hugely enjoyed 'Victoria and Her Kimono' and the humour in Shan's other stories."

—**Peter Carey, two-time winner of
Booker and Commonwealth Writers' Prizes**

"M. Shan, with his domestic ethos is, above all, unpretentious and warm. The sure sense of dialogue and timing is allied with a certain originality."

—**Iris Murdoch, and John Bayley,
professor of English, Oxford University**

"Dr Shanmughalingam is one of the finest short-story writers writing in English today. He is in a class of his own, enriching the genre, in fact nourishing it with subtlety and finesse.

—**Tan Sri Johan Jaaffar, journalist, editor, writer and dramatist**

"The stories in this collection are examples of Shan's special gift of irreverent, insouciant, puckish, trenchant humour he brings so unerringly to aspects of his culture and his years in the civil service. They are such exhilarating social comedy and satire. His distinguishing style as a writer: the vibrancy, wit, irreverence and playful use of language, especially of his portrayal of those irrepressible Jaffna Tamil dowagers."

—**Catherine Lim, author of five novels
and ten short-story collections**

"*Marriage and Mutton Curry* is a remarkable debut short-story collection, introducing a fresh, original, satirical eye cast upon a minor ethnic tribe, the Jaffna Tamils, in a multiracial nation of multiplicities of ethnic tribes. The stories are compressed, their humour lightly deadly, and I welcome and celebrate the collection's recovery of this almost-lost tribe for Malaysian literature."

—Shirley Geok-lin Lim, award-winning author of *Among the White Moon Faces*

"Shan's stories are wickedly very funny; in particular, the stories about the Kandiah family, of Ceylon Tamils. He observes them with a tolerant, forgiving eye, aware of their all-too-human foibles."

—Robert Yeo, author of poems, plays and a memoir

"I enjoyed the humour of Shan's stories very much and his eye for irony. I think his short stories work because he is so pithy."

—Dipika Mukherjee, author of *Thunder Demons*, long-listed for the Man Asian Literary Prize

"It's been quite a while that I enjoyed humour in Malaysia stories. But Shan's is a humour that is full of everyday irony, and therefore very humane and down-to-Malaysian-earth. His end-of-story surprises are done with sensitivity and well-hewn skill."

—Muhammad Haji Salleh, poet and recipient of the Malaysian National Laureate

"Dr Shan writes of the Malaysian Jaffna Tamil community with a light, often humorous touch, deftly capturing the syntax and cadences of his subjects' speech, but this light touch disguises a sharp satirical bent and much trenchant commentary on social and family dynamics."

—Preeta Samarasan, award-winning author of *Evening Is the Whole Day*

Epigram Books UK
First published by Epigram Books Singapore in 2018
This Edition published in Great Britain in May 2020

These pieces were originally published (in slightly different form) in the following places:
"Victoria and Her Kimono", *Asylum 1928, and Other Stories*, Fish Publishing, December 2001; reprinted
    in *The Merlion and the Hibiscus: Contemporary Short Stories from Singapore and Malaysia*, Penguin, 2002
"Half and Half", *A Subtle Degree of Restraint, and Other Stories*, MPH Publishing, November 2011
"Birthday", *ISIS*, Oxford University, 1977, reprinted in *Malaysian Short Stories*, Heinemann Asia, 1981;
    reprinted in *Malaysian Short Stories*, Maya Press, 2005
"Rahman's American Visitor", *New Writing 4*, Silverfish Books, 2004; reprinted in *ku.lit: Asian
    Literature for the Language Classroom*, Vol. 2, Pearson Education South Asia, 2014
"Naming Names", *Ripples: Short Stories for Secondary Schools*, EPB Publishers, 1992
"His Mother's Joy", *New Writing 2*, Silverfish Books, 2002; reprinted in *25 Malaysian Short Stories: The
    Best of Silverfish New Writing 2001–2005*, Silverfish Books, 2006
"Flowers for KK", *KL Noir: White*, Buku Fixi, 2013; reprinted in *TRASH, A Southeast Asian Urban
    Anthology*, Fixi Novo, 2016
"Free and Freed", *Collateral Damage: A Silverfish Collection of Short Stories*, Silverfish Books, 2004
"Rani Taxis Away", *Readings from Readings 2: New Writing from Malaysia, Singapore and Beyond*, Word
    Works, November 2012

Epigram Books UK
53 Baker Street
London, W1U 7EU

10   9   8   7   6   5   4   3   2   1
www.epigrambooks.uk

MARRIAGE and MUTTON CURRY

M. SHANMUGHALINGAM

EPIGRAM BOOKS
SINGAPORE · LONDON

For Felicity Jones, Shirene & Rohan Shan,
Akaash, Emile, Noah & Kamal Bairamov

CONTENTS

ROYAL FOREWORD

Dato' Dr M. Shanmughalingam's short stories and poems have been published previously in 37 national and international anthologies. I am delighted that he has now brought together in one book 15 of his best short stories, including six new ones.

I have known Dato' Dr Shan since our Oxford days, when I was reading Philosophy, Politics and Economics and he was studying for his D.Phil in Political Economy and Government. He was already enjoying success in the very different world of literature back then, when he won second prize in the Oxford University Short Story Competition, judged by the esteemed novelist Iris Murdoch and her husband, Professor John Bayley. So I was not at all surprised when he went on to gain further acclaim in the literary arena after Oxford.

While I proceeded to study and work on our country's economic history, Dato' Dr Shan has focused on illuminating our historical experiences through his colourful stories, the settings of which span the colonial period, the Japanese Occupation and the formative years of our independence. Such fictional accounts are just as important for understanding our history as non-fictional approaches, and the individual lives and specific events that are described in these stories convey most effectively the growing pains and the joys of a young and developing Malaya, later Malaysia.

The stories in this collection are set within the Jaffna Tamil community to which Dato' Dr Shan belongs. This small diasporic community, originating in northern Sri Lanka, has always punched well above its weight in Malaysia and beyond, producing the first education minister in Malaya and two deputy prime ministers in Singapore; countless highly regarded professionals from doctors, lawyers and engineers to key members of the Malaysian civil service; female freedom fighters and social activists on women's rights, education and social justice; sporting heroes; and literary figures such as this author.

But while the stories appear on the surface to be about the Jaffna Tamil community—depicting the hopes, dreams and foibles of its members alongside its foods, cultural and religious practices, and even its names—the insights they provide on the human condition go well beyond the experiences of any one ethnic group. The careful diligence of the wife trying to protect her less discreet husband during the Japanese Occupation, the pride of the civil servant in his prospective promotion, the frustrated ambitions of a dutiful housewife—all these illuminate universal emotions, struggles and relationships, cutting across the experiences of any one group to speak to us all.

It is this aspect that I value the most in this collection, along of course with its humour. Our most human pretensions and weaknesses are depicted with a light and humorous touch that shows the author's deep empathy and his acute understanding of the human condition. Dato' Dr Shan laughs with, rather than at, his community, whose nuances, little jokes and colloquial terms he knows intimately. He pokes gentle fun at the civil-service careerism and the boastful Tamil mothers seeking for their daughters upward mobility through marriage, but all are portrayed sympathetically, with an indulgent rather than critical eye and to great comic effect. As the writer and professor Shirley

Lim put it, tear-jerking is easy, but a special talent is required to write with humour.

Medical doctors appear a lot in the collection, seen as prize catches in marriage by ambitious mothers, and generally as the wealthy saviours of the sick and the unwed. Food also features widely, with domestic scenes revealing in detail the daily lives of the female characters as they buy ingredients, prepare dishes for their husbands and families, teach neighbours how to cook, and make gifts of food to potential suitors or their families. Apart from making one's mouth water, some of these dishes have particular symbolic significance, including kolukattai with gula Melaka syrup, dodol, and the mutton curry that gives the book its title. Characters and situations are brought to life through the smallest details, with images such as folded arms, or the hem of a saree sweeping across a woman's face, loaded with meaning.

But there is also a more serious side. The stories provide rich historical and cultural insights into issues from the patriarchal constraints on women to the resistance to colonial and neo-colonial institutions, such as in the stories about foreign officials whose missions to the country are thwarted by cultural differences. I found the stories of Rasamah/Chelvi and Indra/Thangachi particularly compelling for their sensitive treatment of familial struggles, betrayals and disappointments. Even the horrors of the Japanese Occupation are effectively conveyed through the same combination of the author's detailed description of a specific individual's experience, his deft characterisation and, above all, his use of humour.

Dato' Dr Shan is a master storyteller, as this collection amply demonstrates. His distinctive voice and high quality of writing make for a most pleasurable, rewarding and stimulating read.

HRH Sultan Nazrin Shah
Istana Iskandariah, Kuala Kangsar

VICTORIA AND HER KIMONO

The Tiger of the Victoria Institution, Albert Ramanan, was so busy slapping Mohamad Ali in the school hall, he did not realise that Queen Victoria's portrait had slanted to the left on its own. In all the years since the school opened in 1893, this was its first tilt; rightward might have been a good omen, but was this sinister?

The Victoria Institution sat on its throne at the top of Petaling Hill in Kuala Lumpur.

Ramanan, the Form 1 English master, was tall, dark and "hands on!" "Hands for slapping misbehaving students' cheeks and shaping their characters" rather than for "hail and well-met shaking". Ramanan, with his Junior Cambridge Certificate, bragged that all of the VI's headmasters, past and present, had been Oxford and Cambridge graduates. Each morning he hummed the school song, based entirely on "Gaudeamus Igitur" from Oxford, as he steered his motorcycle through the school gates. The VI's crest, he reminded his students, displayed both its origins and its ambitions for its pupils with the tasteful light and dark blues of both British universities. Ramanan told his students never to ask anyone which school they came from. If they were from the VI, they would tell them on their own. If they were not, then one should not embarrass them. He added, "You can tell a VI teacher, but you can't tell him anything."

He strode into the school in his topi, closed coat, silver buttons, white long-sleeved shirt and long trousers, starched till they seemed painfully brittle. In his coat pocket were red, black and blue fountain pens and sharp 2B pencils to match his chilli-padi temper. He never loosened his collar, even when perspiring under the creaking ceiling fans. As an old boy, he considered his conversion from student to teacher a case better than a thief turned policeman.

He was a proud son of the enterprising offspring of Jaffna Tamils in Ceylon. Ramanan told his headmaster, Dr Lewis, that his forefathers had crossed the seas in the late nineteenth century on the strength of a telegram: "Work Arranged. Come." Armed with an English education, these workhorses helped to develop this land of coconut milk, rubber-tree milk, tin and tinned milk, buffaloes', cows' and goats' milk. They manned the junior ranks of the education, public works, railways and telecommunications departments, for the honey of a regular salary, government housing and a pension that nourished pride more than the family.

Among colleagues in the staff room, Ramanan felt he was a man among men, a chap among chaps. A familiarity with the school developed while both boy and man, the esteem of his colleagues, and an unchallenged knowledge of his family's role within the engine house of State gave Ramanan the confidence to regale the headmaster with a flood of anecdotes. Headmaster or not, Dr Lewis had never been a student of the Victoria Institution, had never known the secret lore passed on from generation to generation of boys, and so could never really know the school he was supposed to lead.

Ramanan smiled, overhearing the seniors telling his new class that "Ramanan Master was fierce, to be approached with great caution, if at all". He introduced his class to *Oliver Twist: Tales Retold for Easy Reading* by the world's greatest novelist, Charles Dickens, "who, of course, was British".

So grateful were the students that they nicknamed him Bill Sikes. Ramanan got wind of this but had no confirmation of it. Along with the normal run of essay topics designed to occupy if not excite the eager pupil, such as "My British Holiday" and "My Family", one day Ramanan offered "My Pet".

Mohamad Ali, nonetheless inspired, began,

"My pet is a dog named Bill Sikes."

That first sentence confirmed Ramanan's suspicions about his nickname, more so since dogs were anathema to his Muslim pupil. Ramanan heard his cheekiest student betting out of the side of his mouth on whether the teacher's collar button would burst before Mohamad Ali's collar parted company with his shirt.

Ramanan charged up to Mohamad Ali and lifted him bodily from his seat.

"Oohh, your dog's name is Bill Sikes! I'm going to your house straight after school today. I shall call out for Bill Sikes just once. If your dog does not dash out answering to that name, God help you, I shall give you a good flogging. We shall see whether you survive it. No criminal can survive my rotan." Ramanan hit the cane on Mohamad Ali's desk.

"No, sir. The dog won't come out, sir."

"Why not?"

"He died last night, sir."

"Then show me where you buried him."

"Cannot, sir."

"And why not?"

"He is missing, presumed dead, sir."

"A bit of a rogue you are."

Ramanan pictured his former British teacher caning his classmate who was once caught reading comic strips between the pages of his book. He twisted his ruler around the flesh on Mohamad Ali's buttocks as the latter winced, veering away from him.

"How old are you?"

"Thirteen years, sir."

"Thirteen years of what?"

"Thirteen years of wasted life, sir."

The Tiger was satisfied.

The nickname Bill Sikes died as promptly as the dog did, never to be heard of again. Ramanan felt that Queen Victoria would have contemplated proudly, if somewhat askew, her Tiger's victory.

The British Empire marched on as Ramanan sat marking exam scripts in the classroom in the humid morning air, nodding approvingly at the neatly knotted string holding each script together—top left corner. But even the best regulated of empires was not without its insurrections. Index No. 67 had knotted his answer script on the right such that Ramanan could not turn the page over. He asked his class monitor to locate the culprit. Several minutes later, Index No. 67 turned up.

"Careless wretch, what's your name?"

"Liew Fook Yew, sir."

Ramanan jumped up, kicking his own chair to amplify his rage. It was an act he had picked up from his wife.

"Are you scolding me or telling me your name?"

"No, sir! Yes, sir!"

"Make up your mind. Is it yes or no?"

"No, sir, I'm not scolding you, sir. Yes, sir, that's my name, sir."

"Cross your arms, hold your ears and recite 'tie knot on left hand' while doing twenty squats and sit-ups. You can have the honour of bringing my chair back, and then get lost."

"Sorry, sir. Thank you, sir."

Ramanan knew better than to ask Liew to clarify his second double-barrelled answer. He felt Liew would have been a nightmare witness in court with his "no" and "yes" answers.

The Tiger was content to send Index No. 67 packing while he continued with his marking.

It transpired that Fook Yew was not only the possessor of a potentially disturbing name but also the son of another VI teacher. For this reason alone, Ramanan pretended not to overhear Fook Yew telling his classmates a supposedly true story about one of his uncles, which confirmed Ramanan's suspicion that Fook Yew was well aware of the implications of his name.

"My uncle is a very rich man. When he was in a restaurant in New York, he brought his own chopsticks to eat spaghetti." Fook Yew's classmates started to giggle, anticipating a lascivious punchline. Ramanan lingered at the door to the classroom, reluctant to interrupt the storyteller and himself not a little interested in the outcome of the New York visit. "Well," continued Fook Yew, "a waiter quickly came up to the table and asked my uncle, 'Wanna fork, sir?'" Fook Yew drawled out the phrase in a style learnt from watching cowboy films at the cinema. "Yes, what next?" his audience chirped as Fook Yew paused for effect before delivering his punchline. "So my uncle says, 'Me Malayan. Eat first. Then fork.'"

Ramanan noisily turned the door handle leading into his classroom and the gaggle of small boys scattered. Although a tyrant in his classroom, Ramanan remembered with affection the Masonic rituals that bonded small boys, sometimes for life.

The next morning, Ramanan announced the annual athletic sports meet. He said every boy, except those with wooden legs or medical certificates, had to run in the qualifying rounds, starting with the cross-country run.

"Your MC must come from a medical doctor. A certificate from our headmaster Dr Lewis, who has a PhD, won't do."

Even the qualifying rounds before the actual sporting events left the boys puffing, as masters on bicycles relentlessly followed behind the sweating students, ready to wield an encouraging gym shoe against any backside that showed signs of wilting. As Ramanan announced the torture schedule for the following day, war was definitely in the air. The boys had prepared for it the best way they could, and as Ramanan came to the end of his list of events, a chant arose in unison in the assembly hall.

Theirs not to reason why
theirs but to do and die.
Mr Ramanan to right of them
Sports Master to left of them
Headmaster in front of them
Volley'd and thunder'd.

Although privately amused by this show of independence and most definitely proud that they had chosen to assert themselves through a poem that he himself had taught them, Ramanan knew that his position as teacher, indeed, as a master, required a show of aloof indifference. A resounding shout of "Sure die lah" concluded the boys' adaptation of Tennyson's war epic with their own take on "The Charge of the Light Brigade". But they had learnt an important lesson in solidarity, as even Ramanan's unmovable collar stud could not cope with caning the four hundred.

"So," he said, suppressing a smile with difficulty, "I expect you have all heard of people dying in their sleep? My advice to you is not to go to bed tonight."

Attendance for athletics the following day was 100 per cent.

Ramanan was proud of "his" boys as much as he was of "his" school and relished their many sports victories, which was one of the reasons he drove his charges so hard. As it happened, the only major Victorian defeat was further proof of the value of joint action.

The VI boys, brought up by Ramanan in the English tradition of understatement, cheered their team the way he did:

"Jolly good, good show, come on boys, well played."

Ramanan and the cheerleaders were taken aback by the thundering yells echoing around the football stadium.

MBS! MBS!

Rah! Rah! Rah!

MBS! MBS!

Rah! Rah! Rah!

Zim! Boom! Bah!

Raaa—aah!

The cheering was relentless throughout the entire match. The MBS team was inspired.

Apparently, the Methodist Boys School had a new American teacher who had taught the boys the value of cheerleading, albeit strictly with no girls. The gentlemanly VI team and its supporters stared at their blancoed Fung Keong canvas shoes.

Ramanan grumbled to his wife about the VI's defeat due to aggressive unrefined behaviour and the students' whining about travelling third class.

"Could it be a sign of worse things to come, Ayah?"

Mrs Vickneswari Ramanan was as fair as Ramanan was dark. Vickneswari glared at onlookers who called them the kopi-susu couple. She applied talcum powder to her face as soon as she woke up. She ringed fragrant white jasmine flowers around the bun on her black hair. Ramanan, who attributed his grey hair to his wisdom, called hers "India-ink hair with white border". She wore sarees and sarongs in riotous colours, in sharp contrast with Ramanan's perpetually whitewashed wear. She had such exquisitely beautiful handwriting that she became the calligraphic gladiator of the whole community. Relatives and neighbours sought her out to narrate their messages through her. She added her own garnishing, provoking laughter in the reader not intended by the narrator.

His children were terrified of his temper. Vickneswari reassured them:

"Don't worry if he loses his temper, I will find it for him. Then I'll remind him not to be so careless the next time."

Vickneswari's passion was Tamil films. After lunch, she would grab any one of her children nearest to her by the wrist and announce, "I am taking you for a treat at the cinema. Hurry, the film is starting."

She could walk right into the middle of a Tamil film and tell instantly who her hero was as he would be dressed in traditional Indian attire and speak only in Tamil. He was the most polite to his mother. He was the first to offer his blood for transfusion. The chief villain, in contrast, sported Western suits even in the hottest midday sun like her Ramanan, peppering his conversation with English words. Vickneswari said if she were acting in the film, she would pummel the crook who was rude to his mother.

"He was so westernised, Ayah," she rubbed it in.

Ramanan teased her yet again. "Victoria, if you are not reading world history or doing pooja, you're at the cinema or telling me the entire plot. Are you rehearsing to be a Tamil film actress?"

She pounced on the opportunity: "You have never seen a Tamil film. You westernised 'rice-bowl Christians' don't appreciate our own culture. Our grandparents in Jaffna converted to fill their rice bowls and to get scholarships in Methodist mission schools in Ceylon. Although most people call me Vicki for short, you insist on calling me Victoria. You speak Tamil with a nasal British accent. Do you want to be a karupu sutu vellai kaaran, Ayah?"

Ramanan buried his face deeper in the literature scripts.

Ramanan was with his colleagues in the staff room.

"This rain reminds me," he began during a particularly heavy downpour, "of the telegram my father sent to his district officer. 'Rain so heavy *stop*. Whole district flooded *stop*. Bridge absconded *full stop*.'"

Dr Lewis replied, "Quite, quite," turning a third "quite" into a cough before remarking that he had rugby results to check.

Ramanan was unsure whether Dr Lewis was praising his father's wit or criticising his choice of vocabulary.

"But that," continued Ramanan, clearly in no mood to let the headmaster depart until he had completed his repertoire, "was less astounding than when he requested compassionate leave. 'Wife died *stop*. Request emergency leave to go to the crematorium to fire her up *full stop*.'" Dr Lewis once again decided on a forward defensive stroke, but assuming three "quites" to be sufficient for one over, played, "Indeed". "And that," continued Ramanan, clearly preparing himself for a fastball, "was itself nothing compared to his altercation with an expatriate officer in the federal treasury. This fledgling questioned my father's request for boots for his staff as part of the Malaria Eradication Programme with the retort, 'Does your department propose to stamp out malaria literally, then?' But was he a match for my father's quick reply? 'Needed for eradication of sarcastic Treasury officials, who should be stamped out, literally.'"

Finally, Dr Lewis knew how to play the stroke. "Wonderful Ramanan, old man. Your father sounds an admirable character." Proud of the praise, Ramanan hardly noticed that the headmaster was saying this as he backed away and turned towards the staff-room door.

Ramanan saw one teacher waving to him to carry on.

He began speaking about his father's system of grading leaders. "Well-above-average ones were ranked…Able Men."

Dr Lewis returned to the staff room dangling a set of car keys at Ramanan.

Another teacher nudged Ramanan on, and hearing Dr Lewis admit he hadn't heard this story, Ramanan continued that these Able Men were differentiated by the lengths their titles' first vowels were stretched.

An Able Man ranked higher than a mere Mr Able, thus starting the double A rating above the A. An even more Able Man rated triple A as the first vowel was stretched to an "Aaable Man". You lent emphasis by raising your eyebrow and head higher the more able the leader was. Among the triple As there had to be one supreme one. Since there were no stopwatch recordings of which of the triple A Aaable Men this was, there was a unique title for him. The greatest of all the Aaable Man was crowned a "Cape—aaable Man".

"I hereby dub you a Cape—aaable Man. You are the best teacher in the school. Since I'm returning to England shortly, you should have the privilege of buying my Jaguar at a discount," Dr Lewis told Ramanan. Ramanan could picture Vickneswari's mocking smirk, knowing the Anglophile in him could not refuse the offer. When he got home, Vickneswari wrung her wrists, saying his entire savings would be sailing away in his principal's steamer. Ramanan wished that Vickneswari would listen to him the way his students did. Apart from the headmaster's, his were the only hands that had ever held its steering wheel. Although she could drive, his wife was allowed in the car only as a passenger. Driving the Jaguar made him feel he was "headmaster on the road", even though it drained his purse.

In late 1941, Ramanan, his colleagues and students were summoned to the school hall. On hearing that the Japanese armed forces had moved through Siam, he imagined the British repelling them at the Siamese border. When his colleagues said that Japanese troops had commandeered bicycles from Malayans and ridden south, he replied that he had never heard of any military invasion propelled by bicycles. Ramanan refused to believe the news over the broadcasting system and swayed on his unsteady feet as he looked up at Queen Victoria's portrait lurching farther left. He gazed out at the dark grey sky, shuddering with each thud of thunder, thinking about the clouds of war that had gathered over the Pacific.

Ramanan told them that he had found a letter in Dr Lewis's drawer when he was advised to get a spare key to his car. It read that the British assumed that any external attack must come by sea from the south. His colleague, Encik Samad, said the Japanese had used strategic thinking and come by land from the north. Ramanan replied that Lieutenant General Arthur Percival had said in Singapore that the British would push the little yellow men back into the sea.

On 12 January 1942, the Japanese occupied his hometown, Kuala Lumpur. The VI was chosen as the HQ for the Kempeitai. Ramanan was the last of the teachers to pack the books from his class and tie the bundle with strings from the school carpenter's shed. He stood in the hall watching a Japanese soldier replace Queen Victoria's portrait with Emperor Hirohito's.

He ferried home the load of textbooks and lesson scripts he had been ordered to set on fire. He kicked open the back door and the pile toppled over for Vickneswari to carry inside. Ramanan slumped into his chair, complaining to her about Colonel Watanabe Wataru's order that Malayans who had long submitted to British rule and "indulged in the hedonistic and materialistic way of Western life" must be taught seishin and trained to endure hardship to get rid of this. Ramanan's face felt hot reading Colonel Watanabe's decree that the English and Chinese languages were to be abolished in all schools. "Dr Lewis was lucky to have escaped as the rest of us male staff have to undergo this," Ramanan said, putting aside the half-completed English examination question-and-answer scripts.

Ramanan and his male colleagues from the VI were forced to attend kunrenjo from 6am to 9pm, where they were taught to live and breathe seishin. With no boys on whom Ramanan could dissipate his anger, it was the paper of Colonel Watanabe's warning that took the force of his hand. "Look at this." Smack. "Trainees who have no seshin," smack, "count for nothing in this world." Smack, smack. "They must never give up on anything." Ramanan's raised hand paused above the paper as his eyes went to where his books lay piled in one corner. "Well, at least not everything he says is wrong," Ramanan reluctantly admitted, and let his hand fall to his side. Vickneswari smiled as she watched Ramanan's anger ebb away.

While Ramanan was depressed by the English language vanishing from the school curriculum, Vickneswari was rather unexpectedly raised up by her love of cinema. Ever since the cinemas started showing Japanese films, she had been going to see these as well. However, without the usual markers of dress and the treatment of parents to guide her, and since all the characters seemed to shout at each other, Vickneswari had no choice but to learn Japanese to be able to follow the action on the screen.

"Nippongo is the new way to pretend to go." Vickneswari turned the pages of her Japanese grammar book. She told him that since the cinemas screened Japanese movies, she'd be glad to tell him the gist of them if he were to come along with her. Ramanan replied that he barely had time to see movies and if he did, he would see only those in English. Vickneswari smiled to herself.

"And where do you think you can see a film in English now?" she asked. "Maybe at your old school? Why not go and ask those nice Kempeitai to show one?" Almost at once she regretted her sarcasm, knowing how much her husband had been hurt by these events.

As Ramanan walked dejectedly from the sitting room, Vickneswari started hiding his English books beneath her Tamil novels and cinema magazines. Tucking a copy of *A Treasury of English Verse* beneath *Indian Movie News*, Vickneswari thought to herself, "So what is so different about the way we shall live? Are tapioca, cow herding and petty trading new to us? Perhaps a period of abstinence will do us well, as long as it ends before too long."

Vickneswari's practicality continued to protect Ramanan from his dangerous attachment to all things English. She even reminded him to remove all the currency in his wallet that portrayed the image of King George VI. Protesting, Ramanan folded the bills into tiny squares and placed them in the box of used stamps he kept ready to add new denominations to his collection of stamps of the British Empire. As he dropped each folded bill into the box, Ramanan spoke his elegy to it. "I will take you out and use you soon. A Straits Dollar is not a used five-cent stamp to be pasted in an album."

When Vickneswari told him that even the stamp collection must be hidden, Ramanan told her that she should worry about much worse news ranging from the death railway in the north to the reign of terror with the Kempeitai informers, torture and imprisonment for the wide range of misdeeds (including the lesser ones of listening to the BBC or failure to bow low enough at Japanese sentry points), shortages of food and the banana currency that wouldn't even buy one bunch of the bananas displayed on their notes. He lifted the blanket draped around his radio. He could hear stations only in Japanese but no BBC, so he turned it off and placed it beneath his bed.

"You thought the British would be here forever. They have retreated. One day the Japanese will also have to withdraw. Don't take them too seriously. We should outsmart them without their realising it. Don't be trapped in the past, my dinosaur Ayah." She squeezed his hand and felt his hand give a slight squeeze in return.

"Play along? For you it's all play-acting or a scene from a Tamil film. Why should I give in to these brutes?"

"I will fool the Japanese into thinking what I want them to think. I'm as bitter about the Japanese military occupation as you are. But instead of knocking my head on the wall, I'm concentrating on climbing over it."

Ramanan continued to give private tuition classes secretly in his house to the pupils, or rather to their parents who saw a future for the English language, whether in the Victoria Institution's British or Methodist Boys School's American. His students included the ubiquitous Fook Yew, a surprising scholar, for these lessons. Ramanan proudly put his stiff teacher's uniform back on, lovingly pressed each day by Vickneswari with her charcoal iron and tapioca starch. Although Ramanan always gave his lessons on his feet, he was careful not to let those feet or his school clothes get too near any windows; Vickneswari quickly closed all windows whenever Ramanan's little group started reciting verse. Ramanan already knew by heart most of the poems he taught, but one day Vickneswari heard the sound of books cascading onto the floor.

"That," she said to herself, "must be my Tamil novels and that," she added, "means my incautious husband is pulling out more literature books."

After the lesson had finished and Vickneswari went in to tidy the room, she confronted Ramanan. "Ayah, our neighbours say the Japanese are hunting down those who persist in teaching English. I am learning Japanese already. I force myself to wear my home-made kimono every morning to hide my hostility toward the Japanese army."

"Teaching English is what I do best. Will you give up your saree and sarong for a kimono permanently?" Ramanan tugged at the kimono sleeve where Vickneswari was stitching crisscross patterns on edgings.

"I'll never give up my saree and sarong. The kimono is a temporary disguise like everything else in life. We need to keep fooling the Japanese so that they can't see the hatred in our hearts. British Malaya was as maya as the Japanese Occupation now. Life itself is an illusion but within it I create miniature illusions with my acting. Why are you so rigid?" Piercing the needle into one part of the kimono's material, she put it aside.

Ramanan inhaled the aroma of the pandan-flavoured kueh from the kitchen as Vickneswari set them out carefully on a woven leaf tray.

"Can I have some?" He held out a saucer.

"Not yet. I made these tapioca cakes to sell." Vickneswari cut out the delicacy into diagonals, wrapping strips of banana leaf around them.

When Ramanan asked her how sure she was that the military would allow it, she said she would barter the kueh for rice and sugar while wearing her kimono.

"Bend in the wind like bamboo, like grass," Vickneswari intoned with a smile, "or crack in the storm like a stiff old tree that won't learn a word of Japanese." Ramanan covered his ear on one side with the empty saucer.

Vickneswari looked at the odd bits of leftover tapioca root from her cakes. She cut them into tiny cubes and made two piles. The larger pile she put in a bowl while she thought about how to turn it into their main meal. The smaller pile she mashed up, and she reached down into an almost empty glass jar from an equally empty shelf. She shook the jar vigorously to loosen the few grains of curry powder stuck on the base and tipped them onto the mashed tapioca with boiling water from a kettle over a bucket of glowing charcoal. Vickneswari regarded the mixture critically and added more water.

"Tonight's soup and tapioca," she nodded, "with the tiniest pinch of salt."

Ramanan came to dinner wearing his white teaching clothes and his old school tie.

"Well," exclaimed Vickneswari, "just look who we have gracing us for dinner. Is it Prince Albert?" Vickneswari covered her mouth with her hand as she chuckled at her own joke. "Maybe the prince should tuck his tie into his trousers though," she added, "or it will flop in the soup and become as stiff as his starched trousers." Seeing that Ramanan was concentrating on his dinner, Vickneswari continued with her teasing.

"And I see that fingers aren't good enough for our two-dish dinner. His Highness needs a fork and spoon. Is it any wonder that your cousin no longer calls himself Kuppusamy but has elevated himself to Sam Cooper BTE—'Been to England'?"

"Ah!" Ramanan replied, "I only use fork and spoon because we have no soap to wash all this chalk dust off my hands. I like to eat white rice not white chalk dust."

Vickneswari heard with pleasure the sound of Ramanan's spoon scraping up the last of his dinner, as it meant that even with meagre rations she could still make a tasty meal.

Vickneswari slipped on the kimono over her saree to check her reflection in the glass sliding doors of the bookcase. The material for the kimono she designed was cut out from an orange floral saree, one that flowed smoothly. She had given her sarees, pavadai and pottu to Fook Yew's mother and elder sisters to help them look like Tamils in order to escape Japanese military harassment. She joked with Ramanan that if she stitched one for him, it would be white.

"Don't embarrass us, dressed like that."

"I'm not rigid or timid. Off you go. Walk your six steps in front and you step first on the land mine. Thank you. In my purse is a picture of my family, but what do you have in yours? Memories of our family's happier times? No, memories of a faded empire with a photo of your dead Queen Victoria. But have you forgotten that Victoria was the queen and Albert only her consort who had to walk behind her, Prince Albert Ayah? So I hope you don't become a white elephant like your white elephant car, more dangerous to us now, hidden in our backyard, than it has ever been with you driving it down the road."

Mention of his car sent Ramanan off on a series of reminiscences—how his love affair with all things English started with the fairy stories he read as a boy.

"It wasn't only with my car that I travelled," Ramanan responded. "With English, I learnt to travel the world and travel through time."

"Oh, so now you are a romantic, are you?" asked Vickneswari. "Perhaps you remember then how your students tried to grow daffodils in their small plots at school after your lessons on Wordsworth. But they raised a fine crop of onions." On a low table, she had placed a vase of red hibiscus arranged into an ikebana display. She reached underneath and pulled out a slim volume. "Here is your Wordsworth, but don't go wandering lonely as a cloud with that book in your hands."

Ramanan cradled the book between his palms. "No," he said. "Hide it again. I know it is too late for me to change but how can I ever put at risk my wife, when she makes such delicious dinners from no ingredients at all."

Ramanan ran his hands gently over the volumes as Vickneswari hid his poetry book back beneath the table. His shoulders drooped as he watched his favourite collection of Shakespeare's plays disappear beneath the cooking recipes, clothes patterns and flower arrangements of Vickneswari's well-thumbed women's magazines.

"Just to be sure," Vickneswari added, as she pulled a sheaf of revision sheets from a tidy stack of newspapers and magazines carefully kept from a time when they could be afforded. She folded the sheets in two and wrapped them in an old bath towel before thrusting the bundle deep down into the sack where she kept her charcoal for cooking.

Ramanan trailed Vickneswari into the kitchen.

He told her if it were a sin to teach English, he would rather remove his false teeth and be speechless. She said it was the language of their colonial past, and he snapped that her Tamil films made it the language of villains. Vickneswari swung Ramanan's old school tie around his neck and hoped he wouldn't be hung by it.

The sirens screeched through their ears. Vickneswari dropped the notepad she was holding to jot notes down from the pages of her Japanese grammar books. Ramanan dashed to latch the open window before switching off the reading lamp. She heard Ramanan curse the darkness of the nightly curfew. Vickneswari rushed to the prayer room and struck a light for her pooja to Lord Ganesha as she spread thirunur across her forehead. She pressed her chest, praying for Ramanan's life and for less stubbornness from him. The last news she heard about the bombing played on her mind. She did not share this with Ramanan. Sometime later, coming out of the prayer room, Vickneswari saw Ramanan sitting in the dark.

"Just think," she addressed the shadow of her husband, "surely when anyone doesn't obey rules, they should be punished? Didn't you do the same when you were teaching?"

Ramanan paused before replying, "But did I force my students to stand in the blazing sun holding a boulder above their heads? And did I chop their heads off if they slacked, as a warning to others?"

"And surely," Vickneswari responded, "it is better to bow low than to lose that head for no reason at all?"

She said it was the war and the military he should curse. The Japanese had opened the eyes of all Asians despite their brutal methods. Of course, it was most risky to go out. They had to pay their respects to every sentry on duty, since they represented the Japanese Emperor.

Both Ramanan and Vickneswari paused and held their breath as they heard a dog barking outside in the darkened street.

Ramanan muttered, "If only that dog had read Sherlock Holmes, then we would all have been better off."

The dog kept on barking until they heard their neighbour, the father of Mohamad Ali, come out of his house and try to shoo the dog away. Frightened, they heard at the same time the ominous tread of soldiers' boots and the click of a sword as it struck the ground. Hushed, they listened to the sounds of soldiers' slapping, hitting and kicking Mohamad Ali's father. The fact that as a Muslim, Mohamad Ali's father was unlikely to keep a dog and he was just being a good Samaritan, even if it could have been explained, would not have impressed the soldiers. Rules had been broken and someone must be punished, but the whole neighbourhood could hear the soldiers forcing their way into Mohamad Ali's house and smashing furniture with their rifle butts. Vickneswari cleared her throat and spat into their bathroom sink. She told Ramanan that the vicious military officer, worse than any dog, had shouted that if the dog's corpse weren't presented before the soldiers in one hour's time, the family would take the place of the dog.

Crouching under their window in the dark, Ramanan and Vickneswari listened as husband, wife and all six children scattered in different directions. As the soldiers stood talking among themselves, Ramanan remembered another group of soldiers he had seen several months ago. He had been walking back from seeing what could be found in the market when a military truck loaded with coconuts passed him and stopped at the crossroad in front. A small group of soldiers jumped down from the truck and began unloading wooden poles from the rear. They hammered these into each corner of the road. Ramanan froze when he saw the flies already swarming around the poles. There were heads speared onto each pole and he recognised a few of the faces. He remembered how the teachers in the VI used to chide their students in exasperation—"We have been trying to drill this into your coconuts for days"—and threw chalk and dusters at them. Henceforth, he never referred to students' heads as "coconuts".

The next morning, with trembling hands, Vickneswari tried to snap off fresh tapioca leaves from the crop in her garden, shaking off the dust-speckled drops of early morning dew as she rinsed them in a drum of rainwater. She ignored the voice she heard from the veranda complaining about no proper vegetables and never any meat. She had heard these things too many times from Ramanan.

"So stubborn," she muttered. "Why complain when we can't change things. It is we who must adapt as best as we can to these changes, no matter how bad they are. At least we haven't been taken away for forced labour like some of the neighbours; even their daughters were taken." She called out to Ramanan, who was on the veranda cleaning his teeth with a twig and charcoal dust, "Just be grateful we have tapioca and rasa velli kilangu. Without that, could we even survive?"

Ramanan stooped over to see Vickneswari dicing one garlic clove before she tossed the flavouring over the bubbling rice.

"I am using a Japanese-style recipe to bring some of their words to your lips."

She told Ramanan she heard on Japanese radio broadcasts that their military were on the lookout for coconuts, chickens to eat and Chinese- and English-language teachers to put to death.

Vickneswari had smoothed tapioca powder over her cheeks and was pinning her hair up over her kimono when the noise of trucks braking outside intruded. She heard curt Japanese male voices. Peering out her window, she saw a military truck loaded with local men, one of whom she recognised as a VI English teacher, stop at their gate.

She grimaced, fearing that this was indeed one of the search parties. Vickneswari rushed to the front gate and clutched it just as one of the soldiers was about to push it open. They both held on, their grips tight and tense. The soldier glared at Vickneswari.

"Today we are hunting for *two*-legged dogs who still teach English."

"Ohayo gozaimasu," she began with a low bow before her pre-emptive strike. "I'd like to know where that useless man is too! He has abandoned me and all my children. If I find him, I'll peel his skin off just for a start. Then I'll…" She picked up a piece of wood lying on the grass. At the top of her voice, she brandished the wood angrily and made threats about what she was going to do to her husband, actions that a stepmother or mother-in-law in a Tamil film would be proud of. "Let me go with you in your truck and we'll search for him together. But I get to assault him first…"

Vickneswari watched the soldier release his hold on the gate and back away from this Japanese-speaking, kimono-wearing, white-powdered woman whose fierce eyes glared straight into his own. The soldier blinked and clutched his cap. In a respectful tone in Japanese, he assured her that he trusted her to punish her errant husband as fiercely as would the Kempeitai and felt confident that he could leave this matter in her capable hands. Vickneswari lowered her eyes and bowed, expressing her thanks for the captain's understanding, although she knew from his youthful face and plain uniform he was only an ordinary soldier. She watched him climb back into the truck, roughly ordering the driver behind the wheel to drive on.

Remembering to take small Japanese-like steps, Vickneswari hurried to the backyard. She looked around, then walked deliberately to the rear of the storage shed, where she lifted the layers of old curtains and sheets that covered Ramanan's beloved Jaguar. Sure enough, sitting rigidly behind the wheel was her husband.

Then, Vickneswari felt he got up in even slower motion than the stars staging a fight or a romantic sequence in a Tamil film. He had removed his false teeth to appear much older. He told her he had practised saying to the soldiers if he was caught: "I've rethireth anth am thoo olth tho theeth Englith."

Ramanan began to say and to do things he had never ever done before. He called Vickneswari "my Queen".

In a torrent, he said, "You...literally saved my life. Forgive me... for underestimating you and not listening to you all these years." And so on.

He also did something else he had never done in his life. The Tiger of the VI staff handed over the keys of his beloved Jaguar to the just-discovered Tigress of Asia.

His newly crowned "Queen" gazed at the keys jangling in his erstwhile fearsome palm still shaking with fear. She turned to his gaunt face without his false teeth for the first time, too.

"The British King nearly died... Long live the Asian Queen...eh?"

"Queen" Vickneswari R. tilted her face upwards to the right. She was amused.

HALF
AND HALF

I'm cramped in a chicken coop because of the colour of my hair. The stink after a hot, damp night is overpowering. The flies and mosquitoes don't seem to mind. The rusty wire mesh makes it feel like prison. My hair and face are covered with chicken feathers, while my toes and heels are sticky with droppings. My ears are pierced by the cackling of fowls. I used to feed them regularly, standing outside, and this is how they show their appreciation! I must tell Amma what I want done to each chicken until this coop is empty.

Why am I here now, although I'm terrified of enclosed spaces? My parents have black hair. Mine is reddish gold, "like our best durian", as Amma says. My skin is fair, while theirs is brown.

When I was a child, my Chinese amah with her black trousers, white blouse and wooden clogs would take me for walks in the Lake Gardens in Kuala Lumpur. The other maids pointed at my skin and light-brown eyes to say, "Wah! European!" One maid said in Tamil, "Vellai sootu vellai karan": white-bottomed white man, as opposed to black-bottomed "white" man. I grinned at her. She didn't know I spoke Tamil too. I learnt that in Malaya all whites are called Europeans, to the confusion of Americans, Australians, South Africans and even the Europeans themselves. The maids spoke in Malay, Chinese and Tamil to the other children and to other maids. But for me they used various types of English. Many spoke through their noses, thinking that that was the only way to get me to understand them. Almost everybody except my family, closest relatives and friends said, "Sure you are European, must be adopted." Amma didn't tell me why I have light-brown eyes, but she said, "Some North Indian babies also got light-brown, not black, eyes after Alexander invaded India the Great."

In my old school, the Victoria Institution (VI to insiders and "Vagabond Idiots" to rivals), our Headmaster and History teacher, Mr Dartford, taught us that our country was first invaded in 1511 by the Portuguese, who stayed until the Dutch attacked us in 1641. "That was before we British rescued this country in 1874," Mr Dartford said proudly, raising his bushy eyebrows. "There must be rogue Caucasian genes floating around here," he added, peering at me and at my brown-haired Dutch–Eurasian schoolmate, Leembruggen. My parents told me that the Portuguese and the Dutch displayed the same bad habit of invasion in their parents' birthplace: Jaffna, in Ceylon.

Late last year, on 8 December 1941, Japan invaded Malaya. The Japanese must have felt it was time that we Asians had our turn; "Asia for Asians," they said. They came in with some military trucks and many bicycles, and took bicycles from the locals without permission. They began hunting the British and Chinese—they wanted to be evenhanded between West and East. So the only Asians to have Asia were the Japanese.

Amma is not amused, particularly when she hears that they are coming towards our neighbourhood. This time, they are looking for people who look British like me. She points at our backyard and says, "Hide, Kandayah." The only place available outside our house is the chicken coop in the back of our compound. That's how I came to be hiding here.

Since my cousin's wife, Hideko, is Japanese, she taught us the only language she knows. Amma greets the Japanese soldiers in her pidgin Japanese, standing by the open kitchen window and speaking loudly so I can hear what is going on. It seems to be going well from the little I can hear. Amma says, "I'm serving you our most precious supply of local black coffee." Then one of the soldiers says that since there are no British or Chinese here, he wants to see what food items he can find to cook later. He steps out of our house into the compound even as Amma tries to distract him with more coffee. I can see him heading straight for the chicken coop where I am perched, trying hard to hold my breath. My skin and clothes are drenched with sweat even though the tropical sun is only just waking up. The soldier opens the coop door. It is shock at first sight for both of us. He freezes, then breathes in deeply before breathing out.

"What are you doing inside here?"

My mouth opens, but no sound comes out.

"Who are you?" he asks.

I say, "I'm nobody." It is his turn to be speechless.

Amma dashes towards him to explain that I am her son.

"Japanese soldiers are not fools. He is a British spy."

Amma pleads with him that I am her very own son and adds, "Once you eat my chicken curry special with potatoes, your tongue will lead you back here again."

He pauses for a moment but shakes his head and turns to me. "Why you try to hide and cheat?" he barks. "You lie you are nobody, you are a spy!" He spits on both his palms before slapping me hard on each cheek.

Nothing Amma says after that can satisfy him. He drags me out by my collar, past flying feathers and flapping wings. I feel I'm no better than a lost mongrel caught by a dogcatcher who is going to put me down. I remain quiet. Amma continues to protest on my behalf, but he continues to ignore her. My King's English won't persuade him in the way I want. I don't let on that I understand Japanese. He drags me all the way to the truck parked at our gate. He and his fellow soldiers lift me and throw me into the back as if I were a bag of rubbish. The bloodstains on the floor seem to be there to prepare me for what is to come. I am blindfolded and driven to what turns out to be the basement of a building. Despite being a local, I had not protested when others assumed I was white. My coffee cup was full of milk. I had gotten away all this while with being a fake white man and now I'm going to be punished for being what the Japanese think is a real "white" man.

I'm in a small cell that makes my claustrophobia even worse than the chicken coop had. The bloodstains on its brick walls are scary in a way that the rust on the wire mesh in the coop had not been. I prefer the old one, even with the chickens. For starters, I'm subjected to two forms of punishment. The first is being beaten with a pole. From the sides of my eyes, I can see that the pole is long and metallic, like what they used at school for high jumps. As the first whack lands on my back, I feel as if my spine has cracked in two; there is an ugly sound and a blistering feeling across my back, but my mind suddenly wanders back. At the second whack, I tell myself that it's doubly ironic as I had been a pole vaulter at school. I remember vaulting to cheers from my house and classmates. I also leapfrogged over the majority of Malayans in many queues during the British colonial regime.

Fortunately, they don't beat me very hard or for very long. I can still feel the bruises and the rawness from the broken skin scraping against the sticky clothes on my back. I'm alive, and it made me remember Amma and my old amah twisting both my ears when they saw the state of my clothes. When only a tiny bit of you hurts, you feel the pain more.

The second form of punishment comes later and is much worse. It is the denial of food. I can hear guards interrogating and punishing prisoners in other cells. Although I am in no hurry for my turn to be interviewed, I'd be happy to answer any questions from them if I could be fed in return for each answer. Unlike Oliver Twist, I don't have the luxury of asking for more as I haven't been given anything that resembles food. Time never moves slower than our giant turtles on Rantau Abang, Terengganu beach, unless your stomach is devoid of any food. When my eyes close, I fall into deep slumber on a stone floor that is as indifferent to my aches as my mattress at home was accommodating to my sensitive skin. I dream of Amma making appam pancakes with their crisp brown edges circling santan, a coconut milk face with soft egg-yolk eyes. I can smell the scent of mint in the coconut sambal chutneys, one green and the other red with chilli. I break the brittle edges of the appam to dip into the bull's-eye. I'm wearing my trademark "elephant squatting on stool" checked blue-and-brown sarong from South India with my white Chinese pagoda singlet. Amma is singing a nursery rhyme, "Three Blind Mice", in Tamil to go along with our meal. Then the rojak man begins the daylong hawkers' procession past our government quarters. The brown peanut sauce, served sweet and spicy, poured on top of pieces of thinly sliced fried tofu, slices of hard-boiled egg, tapioca fritters, shredded cucumber, bean sprouts and cuttle-fish, gives me a burning sensation in my mouth. As if they had planned it, the rojak man is always trailed by the jolly chendol hawker. The chendol, made from green-pea flour imported from Indonesia, mixed with santan, or coconut milk, flavoured with the fragrant aroma of pandan leaves, gooey and gloriously sweet gula Melaka and crushed ice, is perfect for cooling our tongues after the fiery rojak.

Twelve years before the Japanese invasion, when I turned six, Amma went to the headmaster's office in Batu Road Primary School. I stood outside the open door of his office, listening in. Through much of my life I have eavesdropped on others talking. Amma asked for a place for me in the school. He told her the school was full, no place at all. Amma then asked if I could be put on the waiting list. The headmaster asked her to fill in a form. The school clerk noticed me for the first time. He went into the headmaster's office and whispered into his hairy ear. Then he came out to tell me that the headmaster wanted to see me. When the headmaster saw my face, he said his clerk told him that the school had just found a new vacancy that very second. A few minutes later, I was enrolled in the school. Most of the pupils were Chinese. They called me gwailou or "ghost man". When I called them "yellow devil" back, they shouted even louder. I was the odd one out again but I didn't like it this time—worse, being the underdog, I had to keep quiet. My classmate Boon Seng, who had a raised upper lip, said, "Don't worry, I will friend you." He became my best friend, especially because he taught me how to swear in Cantonese. "Wah so nice!" I said. I am grateful to him for life. Whenever I am stressed, I swear in Cantonese. It gives me such relief. Many people say there is no better language for swearing in than Cantonese.

The other boys even turned Boon Seng's name into a swear word. Because his father was rich, Boon Seng always brought sandwiches made with imported tinned tuna fish for his school snack, unlike the egg, tomato or sardine sandwiches that we peasants made do with. So, he naturally became Tuna Boon Seng and from that just Tuna Seng, until some bright spark discovered that if you ran those words quickly together, they ended up as "screw you" in Cantonese. This taunting made Boon Seng's life a misery, and I used to distract them by doing impersonations of our schoolmasters to make the boys laugh with me and not at Boon Seng. Making people laugh was a skill I'd learned from my mother. People avoided her at funerals. She kept a solemn face while whispering jokes about the participants, including the mourners, making those near her guffaw. "Look at those tears from our Sungai Klang crocodiles. They were fighting like roosters only last week." They said she could make the corpse laugh at a funeral. She confessed to me that some avoided direct eye contact with her because even then she could make them laugh from a distance with her mimicry. So thanks to Amma, tuna sandwich and all, we were part of the playground gang instead of its victims.

A kick to my already bruised ribs wakes me up. My stocky interviewer—I hear his name is Hashimoto—tells me that he is going to start stage two of his interrogation. He asks if I have anything to say before he starts. What a thoughtful fellow. Although the invitation is to speak, I interpret it broadly. For some time, I had heard Hideko sing to her baby one of her favourite songs. I begin singing from that recollection, "Kimigayo wa chiyo ni yachiyo ni…"

Hashimoto sits on a stool while I sit on the cold, clammy cement floor beneath him. The moment I start singing the national anthem, he jumps up, standing at attention. He seems confused. When I finish my song, he asks, "How you know Japanese national anthem?"

"I used to hear Hideko sing it to her baby."

"Hideko? Who's Hideko?"

"My cousin's wife."

"Where's she now?"

"Here in KL."

"What is she doing here?"

"Her father is a famous photographer; her uncles were dentists, tailors and bakers here…"

"Father…famous photographer?"

"Oh yes."

"Ah so…very interesting. How you know her?"

"She's my first cousin's wife. My favourite sister-in-law," I add.

His thoughts appear to shift from me and my colour to my sister-in-law and her father. "I don't believe you. I must see her first and ask about her father."

"I can take you to see her," I say, wanting to sound more helpful than I feel.

"No, give me address. You stay here; I go."

"I can help you find the way."

"No need. We have good maps."

He has a point there. They did find their way from Tokyo to Kota Bharu and on to KL without me or any other local tour guide. So, I write down "33 Pahang Road, Setapak". He snatches the scrap of paper and, without so much as a "you are so kind" or at least a "thank you", he vanishes.

On that self-righteous note, I doze off again. I dream I am a chameleon. I am standing in the queue at Robinsons, our most stylish department store on Mountbatten Road, which used to be called Java Street. I am the last one in line, waiting to buy a present for Amma using most of my savings. The salesgirl calls out to me, "Sir, please come in front." I feel as if King George VI were summoning me too, from the framed photograph of himself hanging above her head. She serves me first. Not first come, first served but white come, first served. Nobody protests. It doesn't feel right to me, but Boon Seng materialises at my elbow. He says, "All same same; no change."

Next thing I know, I am at Seng Nam coffee shop in Old Market Square which serves the best golden-brown kaya, a coconut jam, on thick white toast with the crust trimmed off, along with the best local coffee from Ipoh. I am not allowed coffee, but I suddenly remember that I have just got my Cambridge Overseas Senior School Certificate. I am eighteen. I can order as much coffee as I want! The shop is full. I look around for an empty seat. A woman older than I gulps down her coffee and stands up. "Sir, please take my seat." Since she has given up her seat just for me in front of others, she might feel embarrassed if I don't accept. So I take it.

I am grateful to be woken by the sound of a familiar female laugh. I peer out of my cell and blink many times. Am I still napping or just imagining things? I think I see…yes, it is Hideko with Hashimoto and an older man also in uniform. I can see from their gestures that they are looking at photographs of her baby, my half-Japanese nephew. The two military men are making gestures of cradling a baby in their arms and looking wistful.

Hashimoto then turns to see me watching him. He walks over to my cell. "You're a very lucky man," he says.

"That's news to me," I say, trying to behave as coolly as I can from a hot cell, even though I feel like using a few hot words from my Cantonese rickshaw-puller verbal repertoire.

"Hideko says you told the truth."

"She was always particular about that."

He ignores me and says, "She may help save your life."

"Thank you for believing her and me."

"Major Mori say after you sign papers, promise to help us always in future, maybe you won't be punished so severely."

"Oh, help you. How? I have to think deeply about your offer," I say, while inhaling the pungent aroma of Amma's crab curry with string hoppers in my mind. What would Boon Seng say? "Traitor"? Would the crab claws pierce my throat? I wipe the sweat dripping down my forehead and onto my eyebrows. Should I sign? Should I try to be seen as their enemy no longer? Should I try to think beyond my cage? Dare I dream that one day

I might be a different nihonbashi bridge between them and the Malayans, unlike the old British-led order where you had to take advice from the British adviser without any option of ignoring it? Taking advantage of Hideko's presence, I ask Hashimoto about my nihonbashi-bridge idea.

He goes over to consult Major Mori. When he returns, he avoids eye contact with Hideko. He whispers to me, "My major say American saying, 'Winner take all', so who wants to build bridge with loser? Only loser wants."

I say, "Today's winner may be tomorrow's loser. Who can win every time?"

Hashimoto scratches his ear. He seems worried as to how his boss will react. "Maybe my major will punish me if I say you want to argue with him?"

"Can I speak to him directly then?"

"I will ask him." Hashimoto rubs his hands, now looking relieved. He is gone quite a long while. When he comes back, he says, "You can see him but bow very low and don't argue. You are not Hideko."

Oh please, don't make me laugh. It hurts to laugh just now. I am taken out of my cell to see Major Mori. As I enter Mori's office, I see Hideko about to leave from there. She embraces me for the first time ever. The sight of Hideko giving me, a suspected spy, a full embrace while dressed in her traditional Japanese kimono makes Mori and Hashimoto widen their eyes and gasp. They seem dazed. It's worth more to me than all her telling about how much she can vouch for my story. When I am granted an audience, I follow the first part of Hashimoto's advice by imagining that I am standing before the Emperor of Japan. I bow so low that I almost fall over. Major Mori's toothbrush moustache spreads out into a smile. He covers his mouth, which has a gap between his front teeth, with a white handkerchief.

I repeat the message that I had tried to send to him through Hashimoto. Mori's smile begins to shrink before my eyes. He looks up at the ceiling. A chicak looks down at both of us, then flees the scene. Major Mori begins to speak.

"You told Hashimoto that Hideko's father was a photographer. I have seen in Tokyo photos of all the big towns in Ma-rai-ee. Maybe her father took those pictures?"

"Yes, he travelled all over Malaya on his motorbike, whistling Japanese tunes while snapping photos. He must have earned a lot from them. He became rich."

"What was his name?"

"Yamaha."

"Yes, that's his name. Is it a lucky guess?"

"I speak only the truth, sir."

"All prisoners claim that."

Having checked my story with Hideko, this fox is now cross-checking her story with me. To find out how much I know? He is a cautious if not cunning man.

"Your timing is not good. We have just won a major victory in Ma-rai-ee. How can I or Hashimoto or even little you dream of Japanese losing at this time?"

I had, in fact, dreamt of just that; more than that, I had wondered about the consequences for me.

Maybe my empty stomach was roaming around town looking for a sandwich, but despite Major Mori's moustache-bristling presence, my mind starts off on a journey of its own. I begin to recall how my Malay friend Wahab once told me that because everyone thought I was European and therefore couldn't possibly understand anything they said that wasn't in English, I had become a VIIP—a Very Important Invisible Person. I liked "Very Important" more than "Invisible"; at high school, one of our aspiring local gangsters even told me to warn the headmaster "as a fellow European" against expelling students who had family connections with the secret societies. When I relayed this piece of advice to the headmaster, his reply was that the gangsters should come to get him that very evening. Intrigued, I asked why. His reply, "Because I shall be waiting with my Smith and Wesson pistol", didn't seem to be sufficiently diplomatic for the gangster, who spat and told me to Tuna Seng. He must have been at Batu Road Primary School too. Therefore, I know that I have good credentials in bridge building, especially in unsuccessful attempts. But in that case, what might happen if the Japanese were thrown out? Would the Malayans see me as a useful bridge that helped ease their occupational burden, or would it be the British who came back, to whom I would probably very simply be a collaborator?

Major Mori has just confirmed that Hideko's father's photos of Malaya were seen by the Japanese military in Tokyo. Were they deliberately taken for that purpose? If so, will my relationship with Hideko, which she has just pretended to be closer than it really is, boomerang on me? Could the Brits come back and find me guilty because of that? Wouldn't it be ironic that Hideko, my saviour, would then become the cause for British accusations that I was a collaborator? Is it safer to just sit here on the fence? Such are the dilemmas survival presents us with, especially if we are one thing but look like something else.

"I am not thinking of Japan's losing," I lie.

He ignores me and asks, "You sang our national anthem?" Again, the fox is double-checking.

"Yes, sir, I heard Hideko singing it together with English nursery rhymes to her baby, who is my nephew," I say, trying to link things Japanese with things British.

"Do you know the meaning of the words? Our anthem says may the Emperor reign for a thousand years, for eternity. We see Japanese rule over Ma-rai-ee for eternity."

"I am still hoping to be a nihonbashi bridge in Malaya between Japan and all the non-Japanese here."

"You mention English nursery rhymes. You know 'London Bridge is falling down, falling down'? So your British bridge may not stand up for long either."

"My fellow Malayans say you are like the British in one big way."

"Oh, how is that?"

"They say you are dividing and ruling us just like them."

His face reddens. "Ah so, you are so well informed. You agree with them?"

"Half and half, sir."

"Pity, my nihonbashi bridge will look east only to Japan. All, our Japanese way. No half and half. Not even three-quarters ours and quarter others' viewpoint."

"Also, sir," I say, playing my last card. "I speak some Japanese that I learnt from Hideko. Can I be your interpreter and your bridge with all the local groups, sir?"

"Ah, so you speak Japanese too, yet you don't agree with my viewpoint fully." Major Mori sips his hot green tea. He doesn't switch languages to test me. Does he trust me a bit more now?

His eyes seem to follow the steam from his cup up to the ceiling. "I will think about it," he says, pressing his fingers so hard against his bamboo table, I fear it may break.

I think of the time I helped Amma make her heavenly dodol on her bamboo table as she stirred the santan, gula Melaka and flour. While her elbows were swollen and hurting, I was busy licking my little fingers and watching the chicak that seemed to always follow Amma around from its position on the ceiling. There is a chicak here today, too. An omen? A reminder of the chameleon I wish to be to everyone. I am suddenly overwhelmed with a longing for Amma's chicken coop, even the smells, even the smearing of droppings all over my feet. I look up at the ceiling where the chicak is still tik-tikking busily but, search as I might, I cannot find it.

The inscrutable Mori sips his green tea, still thinking.

BIRTHDAY

"I'm going to have a baby," Mrs Santha Gnanapragasm whispered to her husband.

"Afterwards, afterwards, let me finish hearing the commentary lah. West Indies are four wickets down already," the lord and master of the house said, preoccupied. "Vie can't you wait for a little while, ah?"

Just then, someone began to chant about some free gift offer; or perhaps it was a pop song, Santha was not sure. Not one to be distracted, normally, she retreated to her housework. She would wait until the West Indies lost all their wickets. Settling down with her plates, pots and pans, Santha attempted to hum a Hindi tune to herself. She was much too happy to let Gnanam or his cricketing gods upset her.

I hope she's going to be a girl. She will stay at home with me all the time instead of roaming about like all these boys in the neighbourhood. A little more chilli powder for the fish curry. Girls are reliable. They listen to their parents, not boys. You feed boys, bring them up, educate them, but once they start working, they scoot off with some Chinese or Eurasian woman. How very treacherous of them. I think I'll call my little girl Nithi. She will have long, wavy hair like her grandmother. And she will play the violin. Mmm, the brinjals are well cooked. It's almost 8.30pm and Gnanam will be roaring for his dinner. I think I will tell him about our little girl during dinner.

"I say, I'm getting gastritis," Gnanam announced. "Vat, vat curries have you made? You have been in the kitchen since I came home from the office."

Now it was her turn to ignore him in this duet of monologues. She laid the table while Gnanam measured the floor with his feet, chewing on his cheroot.

The first item on the menu was steaming white rice, expensively stripped of all its nutrients. There were also curries of mashed brinjals and lady's finger. Gnanam had eyes only for the fish curry. Reaching out for his regular dose of sour milk, Gnanam attacked the food with gusto.

While Gnanam's fingers wallowed in the rice on his plate, Santha decided to repeat her secret. Ladies, secrets like murder will out.

"You know what, Gnanam, I'm going to have a b-baby."

"Vat—a baby! Very good idea, Santha." As if Santha had just decided to have one and he was in favour of the idea too. Slowly the words seeped into his skull. "I say vie vie didn't you tell me as soon as I came home, ah! You mustn't keep things to yourself like this, you know."

Santha smiled to herself. Gnanam was not so bad without the cricket, his politics or his newspapers. Not oozing with gallantry but attentive nevertheless.

"Can I have the day off, Encik?" Gnanapragasm asked his boss. "My *oif* is delivering her baby today."

"Sure," Encik Nik grinned. "I hope you get a boy. But girl also not so bad. We need someone to look after us when we retire."

When Gnanam reached the hospital he could see the rest of his troupe performing a war dance with their jaws. Towering above the crowd, totemlike but gesticulating and interrupting everyone else, was his father-in-law, Arumugam.

"That fellow is just coming lah. Oi thambi hurry up!"

Gnanam responded to the call of the old buffalo, immersing himself among Mr Arumugam's subjects.

Santha was in the operating theatre. "It's going to be a Caesarean," a nurse hailed Mr Arumugam. "But don't worry."

"Macduff was born that way," said Kandayah, smiling at everyone.

"No!" corrected Mr Chinniah. "It was Alexander the Great."

"I'm sure it'll be a boy!" Mr Arumugam dispensed with all controversy. "He will grow up to be a doctor or an engineer."

"He must get at least a BSc," pronounced Mrs Chinniah.

"My daughter is very stubborn. Insisted on doing Arts. Her father is very disappointed with her. What to do. Our children think they know better than us," said Mrs Chelliah.

"For a boy to do Arts is a complete and utter waste of time. Don't you think, master?" quizzed Mr Chinniah.

"You're completely right," nodded the local Mathematics master. "Arts is for all those morons who cannot understand Science."

Gnanam wished they would stop jabbering but he knew better than to say that. Santha had been feeling a little weak for the past few days. But of course, the obstetrician knew best. If he thought Santha could take it that was all there was to it. As long as Santha was all right and the child was healthy he did not give a damn if it were a boy or a girl.

Mr Arumugam and troupe had been waiting for an hour when a nurse stepped in to whisper to him, "Your daughter's baby is the one we just brought into the nursery with the blue blanket."

"It's a boy!" trumpeted Mr Arumugam.

"A boy, boy," chorused the rest.

"Mrs Pragasm is feeling fine," whispered a nurse, giving Gnanam a broad grin. Santha and the baby were all right. Was he relieved!

"His nose is just like his mother's," said Mrs Chelliah.

"He has got his grandmother's eyes all right," whispered Mrs Chinniah.

"He's even fairer than my daughter," admitted Mrs Chelliah.

"Thirty years I've been in government service and this is the healthiest baby I've ever seen," came Mr Arumugam's verdict. You would have thought he was some government midwife or other.

"You see his eyes…his nose, mouth, his whole face is exactly like his mother's. Boys tend to take after the mother. I read this in a magazine the other day in the USIS Library. I read a lot you know," said Mr Chinniah.

Mr Arumugam felt compelled to let his fans hear his voice again.

"I tell you my grandson will not only be a doctor; he'll be a specialist. One look at his face I know. Just like my daughter Santha, very clever this boy ah? I think he should be a heart specialist. My *oif* has been suffering from heart trouble since the Japanese Occupation. I would have taken up medicine, but my father couldn't afford to send me to college."

"The bugger failed his Standard 8 lah. Who's he trying to bluff?" Mr Chinniah sniggered to Kandayah.

"I expected Santha to get a baby boy. She's such a nice, homely girl. She really deserves a son," said Mrs Chelliah.

Obviously, those with daughters were neither nice nor homely, reflected Gnanam. He remembered Santha wishing she could have a girl. She would learn to play the violin. They would both go to hear her play at concerts and perhaps on Radio

Malaysia too. They would both sit at the front row as they did at the cinema, their eyes riveted on her playing.

Mrs Chinniah was extolling the virtues of women who produced sons. In her previous life, Mrs Gnanam must have been a priest or a very religious person. The baby was an exact replica of Mrs Gnanam. Anyone who saw Mrs Gnanam need not even see the baby.

Poor Gnanam. Nobody bothered about a mere postal clerk. Mr and Mrs Arumugam had donated their daughter to him because he did not smoke or drink. Why, he did not even play cards. They had many daughters, and postal clerks were not supposed to request much in the form of dowry, anyway.

"Can I see you a minute, Mr…er, Kana…Kanapra…"

"Gnanapragasm."

"Well, can I have a word with you?" inquired the Sister on duty.

"Sure."

"I'm afraid there's been a terrible mistake. I'm really sorry."

"What do you mean?"

"We've got mixed up with the babies. Your baby is in Cot No. 13. Can you see a little girl in the pink blanket? That's your baby."

The silence was sudden.

MONEY MAN

There are myriad advantages to being a visiting dignitary holding the purse strings to World Bank loans. For starters, on landing, I am ushered to the VVIP lounge usually reserved for Heads of State. My passport and baggage are cleared for me. I am chauffeured to a suite in the capital's leading hotel, the Merlin, in a limousine with the government crest of two roaring tigers on either side of a shield. I hope the tigers will symbolically protect rather than turn on me.

The downside is the predictably nightmarish protocol. Necessary ceremonies and itineraries full of meetings, dinners and visits to yet another fertiliser factory. As a newly recruited director of the World Bank by lateral entry from a commercial bank in London, and despite a personal preference for the golf course over the guano processor, I have to try much harder to appear eager and please my hosts.

On this occasion, the red carpet treatment is being rolled out for the construction of a dam on the Muda River. Proposals have been made, surveys completed, evaluation visits made, so now it's time for the major heavyweights to give the final nod to big bucks. Of course, few things in life are that simple. There is the need to ensure that our major industrial member countries have a useful and viable project which will bring foreign currency into the bank's copious coffers. On the other hand, as my officers Bevan and Waide have briefed me, the inevitable political element is that the local Treasury uses the Bank's loan conditions to rein in the other Ministries, in particular those under the powerful Deputy Prime Minister and the Prime Minister. As the latter two are not responsible for the finance portfolio, they are not as respectful as the Finance Minister is to international financial institutions such as the World Bank. I am delighted to ease into my programme by meeting our institutional ally first. The files in my shiny briefcase feel lighter already.

The agenda spells out much of the usual, culminating, as appropriate at top level, in a summit with the Prime Minister himself. Waide, my desk officer in Washington DC, said, "Sir, for your first overseas visit as a new director in the Asia Department, I recommend you go to Malaysia. With its Malay, Chinese and Indian populations, it will serve as an excellent introduction to Asia."

"I have never been to Asia, so I'm not sure whether an official visit, instead of a tourist visit, is the best way to get acquainted with a new country."

"Malaysia is a most safe country to help us meet our lending quotas," Waide reminded me.

The Finance Minister of Malaysia is in full spate, the flow of his rhetoric sweeping through the nation's liquidity issues. There seems little opportunity for a break. Not far off, there's the familiar tinkle of teacups and the exotic aroma and taste of Malay cakes in contrast to the regular crunch of Marie biscuits back home. Every act contributes to public health and happiness. I have read that the comings and goings of the fish market or the vegetable stall are absolutely vital to the developing economy. The closure of a factory here, the careful husbandry of crops there. Always newsworthy; the audible pulse of the nation's working heart.

Bevan, my officer in Malaysia has accompanied me to this parliamentary speech; he tells me that the Finance Minister was such a straight arrow during his undergraduate days at the University of Malaya in Singapore that he regularly won the hundred-yard dash, but was equally regularly disqualified for the two hundred and twenty-yard sprint because the latter required the athletes to curve around an oval track.

When I ask for a translation of certain words, I am told that the Minister had spoken entirely in English. True to his athletic past, his delivery rather resembled a speed-train, syllables rushing past to form new and unexpected words, cons-ti-tu-tion became con-shn, mul-ti-lat-er-al-ism mulsm. A man who has no time to waste is an admirable reflection of the Finance Ministry's tight control of every aspect of the economy. However, Bevan relates that Siva, his Treasury contact, is also the Minister's speechwriter and under instruction to help the Minister brandish verbal prowess.

Even amongst the tightly regulated ministerial corridors, the human spirit seeks freedom where it can and the Minister's verbal shorthand offered the imaginative Siva an invitingly open door. Indeed, so Bevan warns me, Siva's prowess is legendary, introducing the longest words possible into each ministerial speech, each word a badge of honour from the Office of Circumlocution, an intellectual antidote to the rigour of research coupled with the burden of office. Siva sees each speech as a challenge, his ultimate victory being the inclusion of the OED's longest word—antidisestablishmentarianism—into the Minister's annual budgetary speech to Parliament. He knows what ministers are made of; those who survive the heckling of hustings and cavils of the Cabinet are hardly likely to balk at a mere eight syllables. The Minister himself takes this eight-syllabic bar fence at the gallop, leaving parliamentary colleagues arguing whether "andelism" is some form of socialist reform akin to syndicalism, or the apotheosis of capitalism, one step beyond monetarism. Only publication of the speech could resolve the issue; never would Hansard be so avidly read. The Minister looks well-pleased with his colleagues' interest in fiscal detail. Bevan tells me that Siva's only disappointment with his job is that the size of his salary does not match that of his vocabulary.

Bevan and I meet with the Minister of Finance at his office in the Treasury at the State Secretariat building, by the banks of the Klang River in Kuala Lumpur—rather smaller than our Thames in London. His double-breasted suit matches his conservative views and his austere office décor with its faded furnishings. His battered briefcase augments the layer of thin carpet with imprints from shoes and chairs. I feel I have time travelled back to the old world.

I start by complimenting him on his persuasive and detailed parliamentary speech, adding that nothing I had heard in my extensive travels had been more intelligible. The colonial flattery, if such it was, is followed by a quick one-two on the priorities of the Bank for *reconstruction and development*, culminating in a straight blow to the chin, "Compared to the poverty one often reads about in Africa or the Indian subcontinent, I'm still rather confused as to why it's so urgent for the Bank to help Malaysia."

Not a knock-out blow, but the Minister visibly reels and as I had hoped, he appears momentarily lost for words. First round to me; I have neutralised the verbal supercharger. I lean back, feeling in my palms the cracks on the old leather seat's arms. Indeed, the Minister mumbles to himself as he clears his throat, scratching his chin with his forefinger. Eventually, he collects his thoughts and comes back to attack. "Mmm, yes, I see your point, but may I ask, is it right that a country, which lives within its means with balanced books and well-managed finances, is penalised merely because of the prefix 're'?"

It is my turn to reel. "Forgive me, Minister, but would you care to be a little more explicit?"

The Minister quickly follows up this weak defence with relentless body blows. "My dear sir," he explains, slowly and deliberately as if addressing a rather slow-witted child, "while we have little need to REconstruct, we are indeed CONstructing. We hope you will help us CONstruct a new dam on the River Muda to help DEVelop irrigation to enable farmers, to double-crop, to provide electricity to villages, to increase their access to markets with a better road; all things, I might add, which our erstwhile 'advisers' consider less important than digging large holes to extract tin and levelling swathes of forest to plant rubber. We are indeed grateful for this exploitation of our valuable resources, which, when we inherited them, have enabled us, by and large, to avoid the famine and poverty that characterise other parts of the global developing world. However, no matter how one might try, it is impossible to cook tin or rubber to make a palatable meal."

I haul myself back off the ropes and attempt to get back on the offensive. "Yes, indeed," I stutter, "point well taken."

"Ah," comes back the response, the Minister tugging his lapels with each hand. "I wasn't President of the Victoria Institution Debating Society for nothing. You'll come to dinner tonight, of course. I'll send my driver at around seven?"

Wrong-footed again, I can only accept the invitation and try to regain my position as a potential source of largesse rather than a beggar at the table, with a few quick comments on the Bank's special interest in reconstruction and development following the devastation of war. I am determined not to let the fast-talking

Minister get out of my grip without a few final jabs. Vigorous nodding by the Minister helps reassure me that I won handsomely on points during our prolonged handshake. I grin all the way back to my hotel until Bevan, more familiar with local customs and personalities than I, informs me that the Minister's nods meant only, "I hear what you are saying", and gave away nothing as to his attitude on what was being said.

As I wait in the lobby of my hotel, an old but highly polished limousine draws up at the entrance at seven precisely. I am dismayed to find that the Minister's house is only a bit less austere than his office. I recognise the worn rugs. Even the waiter looks familiar. Surely that is the chauffeur with a front tooth missing who drove me here? I reconcile myself to a parsimonious evening.

"Our family tradition requires bottoms up on the first glass. I assume you take your whisky neat?" The Minister is all widespread arms and expansive smile. "My father could take down a brace of partridge at two hundred yards after emptying a bottle."

I offer my congratulations on the sheer Englishness of the Minister and his family.

However, far from the expected frugality, a procession of exotic dishes begins to appear before us. My concern that the driver-cum-butler was also the cook was clearly unfounded and the Minister has sensible priorities for staff deployment. First, a chicken dish followed by fish in a sauce. Having read about potential ambush from Asian spices, I venture upon the more brightly coloured items with trepidation.

Mess dinners and political high tables have nonetheless stiffened my culinary backbone, if not hardened my boiled cabbage palate. I soldier on, even with gusto. I am not deceived.

As soon as the first of the sauces hits my mouth, I feel my face turning as red as the sauce and I begin to perspire from the top of my head. My host, courteous to a fault, orders his driver-cum-waiter to put the ceiling fan at maximum while I thankfully down my third glass of water. The fish dish is followed by a prawn one.

I lean back and attempt inconspicuously to loosen my belt. The pièce de résistance is voluminous crabs cooked with a pungency due to, I am told, fermented shrimp paste, a Southeast Asian essential. Whatever the shrimps had been up to, their heat is incendiary. Under cover of my napkin, I undo my belt a further notch, hoping I will remember to re-tighten everything before I stand up, being understandably reluctant to expose my guests to any sight of the emperor's new clothes. Two helpings later, my hand hovers yet again near the belt buckle. The Minister asks if I have dropped anything. I reply that, on the contrary, I have gained immensely from this dining experience. He leans across and confides that this final dish is sago gula Melaka, a specialty of his historic home state, Malacca. I nod in the way I'd seen him do earlier that afternoon as I attempt to reassemble my midriff.

A troupe of dancing girls appears. I think they are delightful until one catches hold of my arm to pull me into the dance space. The Minister also comes onto the floor; for one moment, I think he means to be my dance partner. I must have been picked out for special treatment, but am informed later that ronggeng dancers normally encourage the audience to join in. The Minister gives me a smile of encouragement and takes a Polaroid of me with my arm held aloft like a naughty schoolboy. I turn towards the troupe with far less grace than a shambolic bear woken from hibernation.

My wake-up call the following morning is at six o'clock. My legs, unaccustomed to dancing, ache. As I swing myself gently out of bed, leaning over to turn the radio on, both the radio and my stomach come alive at the same time. Dry toast is all I can attempt at breakfast, weak fuel in the face of a demanding meeting coming up; I hope last night's feast provides the necessary residual energy to sustain the demanding schedule for the day. The lingering melodies of last night's dance music in my ears remind me how relaxed my hosts are. I can glide and sway through the rest of my official visit like the native ronggeng dancers did.

The Deputy Prime Minister, dressed austerely in a grey bush jacket, gives no quarter and fires a starting volley across my bows. "With all due respect, the World Bank is far too slow. Even the turtles on our eastern coast move much faster. Our civil servants have supplied so much data to your Bank that if it had been water to the farmers instead of paper to Washington, they wouldn't have to wait for the Muda Dam at all."

For the next two hours, I am subjected to what appears to be the whole three volumes of the First Malaysia Plan 1966–70. Now, I am used to listening to dry and rambling presentations from the bank's clients and I certainly understand the pride in first-year economic plans, but this ferocious onslaught of facts, figures and projections, with no let-up for questions or clarifications, let alone a cup of coffee, is demoralising.

The Deputy Prime Minister's other ministerial portfolio is rural development. He invites me to his operations room, where he is briefed by his civil servants on the specific progress of development projects spread throughout the country. He informs me that every one of these briefings is tape-recorded. Each week, the DPM listens to the recordings prior to the next briefing to catch any deception by his staff and chase district officers and engineers whose projects are behind schedule. This is clearly a man who means business. What business he means is currently making a huge amount of noise on the lawn outside the office window. A casual glance reveals a large helicopter. This, the DPM explains, will whisk us away so that we can check on the veracity of these reports on the ground and see for ourselves how developed the development projects are, compared, he adds, to progress with the bank for reconstruction and development.

Since the Deputy has taken such a hard line with me, I have to prepare for the worst at my summit meeting the next morning with his boss.

I get back to my hotel room with one thought in mind: this is not a doddle and I need to know more about the pros and cons of the loan and the personalities I am dealing with before the round-up meeting with the Prime Minister. Waide in Washington could fill me in on the loan details; Bevan, the man on the ground here, is best placed to tell me about people. Bevan then tells me a story that allows me to take my measure of the man I will face. On one occasion at Parliament, the opposition leader had thrown a challenge to the Prime Minister and the government benches, saying that they were full of sinners. The opposition leader challenged any of them to stand up if they had not sinned. The Prime Minister then said that he was standing up not because he had not sinned, but to reply on behalf of the ruling party. He said that if the opposition leader had never sinned, the Prime Minister felt sorry for him. There was applause, thunderous from the ruling party's side, and even giggles from the opposition benches. When another opposition member proposed that adulterers should be stoned, the Prime Minister replied that there weren't enough stones in Malaysia to fulfil that objective. So that is my task: master fine detail while preparing to handle an astute verbal athlete.

Even before I can have a cup of tea (or pour a much-needed Scotch), I badger the telephone operator to put through several long-distance calls to Washington. To ensure that the Bank recoups its reputation of being the leading and the most knowledgeable international financial institution in the world, I need more answers than the questions the Deputy Prime Minister had pummelled me with earlier. At two in the morning, I decide that, despite being stared in the face by another early start, I deserve a nightcap, although more modest than that taken by the Finance Minister's steady-handed father.

The hotel's Yardley soap bar is doing excellent work on my armpits the following morning when the water from the shower stops flowing. "What sort of an omen is this?" as my Indian friend in London would ask. Have my hosts gone over the top to show me that the application for a water-supply loan is urgent? I quietly curse the shower head with a few choice recollections from my army days. The water quickly comes back on. Is that my good omen?

My final meeting with the Prime Minister on the following day will certainly be no formality. Rather, it will be the final battleground. My motto as a boy scout was "be prepared". I am so well primed that I shall conquer this little new nation at my peak battle tomorrow, peacefully and with ease.

I arrive extra early at the Prime Minister's office wearing one of my favourite ties: regimental, not old school. I hope to convey a military frame of mind, not one of pals and chums. This appears to be the modus operandi of this institution, as a very military-looking gentleman, with a clipped moustache and equally clipped hair, brushes past me, looking flustered.

"Who was that?" I ask the Prime Minister's secretary.

He replies softly, leaning forward. "Our Foreign Affairs Minister, known for his short hair and shorter temper. I believe he wanted to confront our Prime Minister for publicly contradicting a major foreign policy statement that he had made."

"What will be the outcome of such an engagement of two heavyweights?" I ask him.

"No fire will come out in the meeting," he says.

When I ask him why, he confides, "Our Prime Minister tells me ahead of time to inform the Foreign Minister that our Prime Minister had to leave in a great hurry for an urgent and sudden appointment."

"What if the Foreign Minister doesn't believe you and peeps into the inner sanctum?"

"Our Prime Minister will hide under the desk in case the Foreign Minister peeps in," he whispers with fingers folded over his lips.

I turn this last piece of intelligence over in my mind. Indeed, conserve fire until you have an advantage. This is a strategic thinker I'm about to meet. As I am ushered into the Prime Minister's office, I straighten my tie and throw my shoulders back. I see that he is seated at his desk.

The elephant tusks flanking the Prime Minister's teak desk send me a fearsome message—I had nearly been trampled by one on my recent maiden safari in Africa. Perhaps the Prime Minister can bag an elephant at two hundred yards after downing a bottle of something? I brace myself for the worst. At least there is no tiger skin on the floor. Taking my example from the aggressive Foreign Minister, I shake the Prime Minister's hand and immediately launch into my summary of findings before either of us even has a chance to sit back down.

"Mr Prime Minister, the primary problem with your government's loan applications for development projects is that the local cost is far greater than the foreign exchange component. As you know, the Bank's lending focus is for foreign exchange expenditure.

As for the Muda Irrigation Project, there are a number of issues. Let me elaborate please." I tick off key points one by one, gesturing with the fountain pen I hold in my hand for greater emphasis. The Prime Minister sits reflectively smoking a cigarette, nodding at intervals. He raises his hand suddenly. Is this a sign of surrender? Has my catalogue of facts brought down his defences?

"I usually play golf in the morning." He smiles, removing his cigarette from under the sparse tracing of his moustache before crushing it into the large, overflowing pewter ashtray on his desk.

Might I have misheard him? Where is this non sequitur leading? In order not to lose my advantage, I press on with greater vigour. "We have several standard conditions precedent which your officials have not agreed to yet. Let me give you some examples."

The Prime Minister continues, as if he had not heard me. "Unless it rains in the morning, then I play in the evening. It is too hot to play golf in the afternoon." He beckons to his secretary to roll down the white Venetian blinds indicating the sun is in my eye.

I'm certain that I'm hearing rightly even though I can't believe it. This is not the response I am expecting. Where is the returning fire? Where are the countering objections? I turn to look at the Prime Minister's secretary, who sits by the door taking the minutes of the meeting. He smiles at me. Reassured, I carry on my factual attack, taking my cue from the straight-line running skills of the undergraduate Finance Minister. "Your rural development projects are small and scattered all over the country. If you are seeking Bank support, then we prefer more manageable major projects."

When I pause, the Prime Minister responds at last. "You have met my Deputy and my Finance Minister. Should I repeat what they have told you? By the way, do you take sugar with our

Cameron Highlands Boh tea? I don't. My people say I'm already too sweet. Actually, it is due to my diabetes. Heh heh."

The Prime Minister raises his teacup, which I note is a Royal Doulton Daffodils. I watch the blue–black ink soaking into my white cotton trousers where my sterling-silver fountain pen had hit my thigh on its way from my hand to the floor.

The meeting is clearly at an end. I am left wondering precisely who can only run in straight lines. I need to see the Finance Minister again before I leave.

RAHMAN'S AMERICAN VISITOR

I feel a surge of pride. I have arrived. I swagger in. "The Treasury, Ministry of Finance," reads the polished signboard.

"So shiny! Must be the Brasso," I muse. The hinges and knobs of the classroom door at the Victoria Institution, where I attended two years of upper-secondary school at Form 6, had been waxed with that stuff. I used to comb my hair in the golden reflection of the brass. How different it was from the mud grains of the West Coast beaches on our school outings.

When I first moved to Kuala Lumpur, I had problems adjusting to the sound of buses roaring by. I had grown used to being pampered by wake-up calls from the gurgling yellow-vented bulbuls among the rain trees. As for my parents, our cockerel startled them awake at five. The smell of exhaust smoke from the lorries was a poor exchange for the refreshing air of the padi fields. I don't see many spiders, the sight of which caused my younger sisters to scream for their lives. I prepare myself for a very different environment here.

The building that houses the Federal Treasury is a gem of Moorish and Mughal architecture, designed by a British colonial architect in the 1890s. The rain trees lining the entrance to the Treasury by the banks of the Klang River remind me of my childhood in the kampung. Here, too, the tall trees with their umbrella-shaped crowns shelter trishaw riders, hawkers and their customers from the monsoon rains when man-made umbrellas are inadequate. Rain was an invitation to splash floodwater on one another on our sampan rides to and from school.

"Ada apen man?" The security guard looks up from his seat and stares at me with my new long-sleeved shirt, tie and groomed goatee. He pronounces "appointment" my East Coast way.

"No need appointment, I have a permanent one." I point to the offices ahead. "I'm starting work here from today."

The security guard raises his shoulders, takes a deep breath and holds it so that his chest fills his khaki jacket. I sense that every breath he takes into his uniformed torso reminds him of his own power. He can decide not only who should be permitted to enter but, more important, how long each person should be delayed before being issued an entry pass.

"Mana kad?" the guard asks as he strokes his greying moustache, turning the pages of the new staff list in the internal telephone directory.

I hand over my identity card. He flicks through the telephone directory, running his forefinger down the column of names, muttering, "Abdullah…Abdullah," being deliberately slow about it. "Abdullah, Rahman." It's there, right underneath External Finance Division, and it lists my position as well: Assistant Secretary, Malaysian Civil Service—MCS Officer Grade. The change in his demeanour is immediate. He stands up and salutes.

I acknowledge the guard's salute with a grin. This is the first time in my entire life that any security staff not merely stands up but actually salutes me. This is just the first of the many perks I'll enjoy as an MCS officer. As the guard escorts me to my room, I rub my hands together. My new leather shoes graze these tiles left right, left right, in perfect rhythm.

Is this going to be my heaven on earth? I remove my shoes to twiddle my toes, resting them on the brown carpet beneath my table. My days of fishing and swimming in the river, laughing with my kampung friends and covering my privates with coconut husks after losing my bapa's only set of trousers, which floated down the river, are over. I continue to reminisce about my life in my kampung in Terengganu. Over lunch with my colleagues, I describe our community of poor fishermen and farmers. I read in my books on Malaysian economic history how the developed West Coast produced rubber and tin that fed Britain's home industries, and so, many of my West Coast colleagues now enjoy cushier lifestyles. In my conversations with my newfound friends, I rub in how they had grown up in houses with toilets equipped with Western-style plumbing while my family made do with far less. They snigger and make me feel they look down on me instead of feeling guilty for being much better off materially.

Around the well we shared with our neighbours in the kampung, I learnt about hierarchy. Men, according to their status or age, then women and finally children. Fortunately, sarongs were "one size fits all". I'd share the only one without too many holes in it with my brothers. That did not prevent the shopkeeper in the sundry shop from sneering at me while he wrote down credit items for my family in his long hardcover logbook, seeing me clutch my tiny 555-brand notebook. "All family one salong only ah? Where got time to wash ah?" he'd ask. I talk with Siva, my colleague, about how my siblings and I read by candlelight until we finally progressed to one carbide lamp for the entire family hut.

Each morning as the security guard stands up to salute me, I am reminded how my life has changed. I studied economics at the University of Malaya, just managing a third-class honours degree. All that mugging is finally going to bear fruit. I breeze past the checkpoint, acknowledging the guard's smile with an indulgent nod. I love the executive chair in my office that enables me to swivel from my dark wooden desk to the beige rubberwood bookshelf behind me. Neatly arranged on my desk are "in" and "out" trays, two fountain pens, a black and a red Quink inkpot and an ink-blotting pad. The bookshelf is filled with the "General Orders", "Manual of Office Procedure" and financial circulars. I open the budget estimates, reading the detailed breakdown allotted to each government ministry and department. I wish I could properly inform my colleagues how I increased my scores in economics, mathematics and accounting from 30 to 60 per cent through sheer dedication and hard work. They could learn a thing or two from me. The only reason I don't is because some of my colleagues might know my former school teachers, who may well rat on me about how I used to get punished by being made to stand on a chair and how my classmates used to tease me about my filthy shoes or my not wearing socks.

Within months of joining the Treasury, the under-secretary directed me to handle the Treasury relations with the World Bank in Washington DC. When I excitedly told my mother about it, she said, "It doesn't matter whether you win or lose. Kalah tidak apa, style mau." Yes, it doesn't matter whether we win or lose, as long as we have style. I put on the glossy cufflinks, given to me by my girlfriend upon my graduation. Shouldn't I buy ones with a matte finish like my colleagues? Neither my light-coloured long-sleeved shirt nor dark-coloured trousers has any tear, in contrast to my childhood sarong, which provided natural ventilation.

Back in my room, I clean the oil patches from my trousers, the result of the breakfast I had this morning of roti canai soaked in sambal. I eat it with my fingers. I eat it with relish. Eating with my fingers is not only tastier but also easier, I tell Siva, who in turn reminds me that dark pants are good for covering most stains.

Today is an auspicious day. A representative from the World Bank is coming all the way from the United States to meet me. This is my first visitor from that distant country. I tell Siva that in movies, the orang puteh did all the talking. Siva agrees that they talk about what they want while the natives just listen. He says that they manage to tell their life history in five minutes without the natives speaking a full sentence. I tell him I will change all that today.

Siva tells me that it won't be easy. Only our new Prime Minister can challenge the white man and look east. I say I hope to be a bit like him and to treat today's meeting as a challenge. Setting my right foot forward, I raise the long ruler into the air; silat poses strengthen my mind. I built my strength dragging buffalos with ploughs alongside my father and brother. Next time I shall show Siva a few of my silat moves.

I practise how cool I am going to act when my visitor arrives. I'll pretend to my guest that he is merely No. 23 out of the two dozen or so foreign visitors I receive in my office on this day alone. I can act as American as the next guy. During my student days, I'd seen a slew of Hollywood films. I wonder if I should do the Gary Cooper walk from *High Noon* as I approach my visitor. Combing my Brylcreemed hair once more, my fingers feel sticky. I practise a line I remember from another movie, "Cool, man, cool!" A loud knock intrudes into my accelerating flow of thoughts.

Mr John Malone, loan officer of the World Bank, strides in, accompanied by the Ministry's security guard. I bet the guard has not asked him whether he has an appointment since he wears a lounge suit. That preliminary hurdle is only for lesser mortals who don't wear a jacket and tie in the tropics. I can picture the guard jumping up like my baby brother when he sees bapa returning from the padi field, immediately escorting Malone to my room.

After crushing my hand, Malone sinks into the seat across from my desk with a humph. Two or three strands of his blond hair are matted against his wide forehead. He flips open the lid of his briefcase and pulls out a thick draft loan agreement, on which my future here at the Treasury entirely depends. I hear only one word issuing clearly from his lips: "Facilities."

I am ready for him, Mr Malone Loan Officer of the World Bank. "I am so glad you came straight to the point. You Americans are so direct. Not like the British or us Malayans. We are so slow to warm up. I am honoured to give you a timesaving verbal tour of the Treasury's facilities. You see this telephone?" I wipe fingerprints off it.

"If I dial 99, my peon will rush in. Almost like dialling 999, for emergencies ah? Ready to bring me and you, since you are my guest, a cup of hot coffee with milk and sugar mixed together in advance—we are very advanced, heh heh. If you prefer, you can inhale the aroma from a tall glass of teh tarik or stir the standard three ice cubes into your Ovaltine hot chocolate. My peon will also collect or deliver a file for me, post my letters, buy cigarettes or cash my cheque."

"Yeah, hrrmh, the facilities for…"

"You see, Mr Malone…" I twirl my finger on the dial of my black telephone, "if I proceed to dial 98, my Jaffna Tamil clerk, who is older and much more experienced than I, will pop up with draft replies on confidential subjects or news about important office matters, particularly about who is likely to be sent on transfer and what grade of farewell party he deserves." I turn over pages clasped with a metal grip showing him signed carbon copies of letters to my counterparts. Malone sticks his head forwards like a turtle.

"He will proofread my letters word by word after collecting them from the typists' pool. He is thorough at correcting not only the errors but also the commas and full stops, improving the drafts so that my letters look really good. My signature carries more weight than his. So, I am on top and he is on tap. Our correspondence goes out top, tap, I mean tip-top!" *Great punning, Rahman!* I think to myself, rather surprised by my own wit.

"Err…the facilities." Malone clears his throat again as he shifts in his chair.

"And one more thing…" I hold out my right palm the way policemen control traffic at key junctions, "Should I dial 97, the Chinese steno will glide in here. She will hang on my every word. She won't raise her pencil-lined eyebrows when I conclude my letters with 'I remain, with all due respect, your obedient servant', even though I am one of her bosses. She knows it's only a formality, not a humility." Again, I give Mr Malone a beatific smile. I am on a roll today. "Not to be taken literally at all. No, sir."

"Just one…" Malone dabs his forehead, perspiring heavily, as if he were being interrogated. Looking up at the vents, I rub my palms together.

"Hold your horses, as we say to you Americans with your colourful cowboy history. To think that just a few months ago, I was a mere undergraduate waiting at the bus stop and trying to thumb lifts to the campus. Now I have people under my own thumb. How thumbs have changed." Malone crosses his legs. His eyes follow the movement of my thumb. He closes his open mouth.

"You know how good the British colonials had it here. They had toilets en suite. How sweet. That is one facility I don't have, but my biggest bosses and the Minister do have. If I were given three wishes," I stroke the flower vase on my table, "I would straightaway ask for an attached toilet. In my kampung, my entire family's hut had only one toilet. Fortunately, rural life moves as slowly as a bullock cart. Nature is in tune with the rest of the countryside and rarely calls all of us at the same time. For emergencies, we have open-air toilets in our padi fields."

Malone's face seems to be growing redder by the moment, whether due to heat or something else is unclear.

"Does it surprise you that the British colonials had to be pressured very hard to leave this tropical paradise for tiny flats in London? They call them 'studios' or something. I don't know what photographs or paintings they can do there. Who would give up this Garden of Eden for cold grey winters, queuing and waiting for buses, trains and test tubes or whatever else? Here, they had chauffeur-driven luxury cars and two-storey bungalows, with lawns large enough not merely for tennis but also for football and rugby. Not to mention, enough servants to assemble a football team."

Malone raises his voice, but it comes out so high pitched that it sounds to me like a squeak from the tikus in our padi fields. "Talking about facilities…"

"Relax, Mr Malone. There are several other facilities. I shall name only a few. Our Treasury telephone operators know the telephone numbers of all the Ministries and departments by heart." I lift my telephone directory. "Pick any agency and they'll have them on the line in seconds."

"So," I add, "you have come to the right place to ask about facilities. By the way, Mr Malone, are you here alone, with some loan facilities? Excuse the pun. I picked up both the punning and the borrowing from my jovial but poor mother. As for our chief clerk…"

Malone thumps his forehead with the heel of his palm. He pulls out his handkerchief and mops the perspiration trickling down between his bushy eyebrows. He slams his briefcase on my table.

"Excuse me, Mr Raymond Arab Dollar. Your tour of the facilities is most awesome, I swear. All I really need to know is, where's the nearest toilet? This is most embarrassing, but it is of a somewhat urgent nature that I ask."

"Aah?"

Mr Malone's forehead begins to crease with pain. Sweat runs down his already florid face in streaks. He paws his stomach and re-crosses his legs, looking for all the world as if he were ready to explode. Indeed, I suddenly realise, he wasn't kidding, as the Americans might say.

"Oh, those facilities?" I point in the general direction of the toilet, befuddled. Malone charges out. I bury myself into my chair. There goes all my brilliant strategy—I had planned to set him off balance by talking first—to gain the upper hand, as the Americans say. Instead, with this one surprising gesture, he has regained control of our negotiations over the amendments to the loan facilities that I had planned to discuss with him. Was it an act? I mop my forehead just as my American visitor did.

I feel sick. My first negotiations, all these expectations riding on me, all these hopes I had of myself, and I might have blown it. The taste of the roti canai and curry I had for breakfast rises in my throat. I have to recompose myself, figure out my next move now that Mr Malone has derailed my spectacularly planned delivery.

Then I, too, head for the toilet.

SEEK AND
SHALL YE FIND?

I smooth the ends of my moustache and smile. Everything is going perfectly for me. My bosses at the Treasury have written favourable reports about my performance, and I am due to be promoted from my Time-scale appointment to a permanent Super-scale post.

If there's one thing better than being Superman, it's being a Super-scale-man. My father would agree; a policeman in British Malaya, he became a watchman at a commercial bank upon retirement. My God, he symbolised the bank's motto: "Big, strong and friendly." A good man who did a great job and who, yes, was later upgraded to security officer.

I've stressed the word "officer" on purpose because my father received all these without approval from the Treasury or the Public Service Department. I, his son, am the first in our community who will be promoted very soon to a Super-scale post in the Treasury. I can look down on any bank manager after my promotion. Why, even Taj, my cousin the doctor, after all those years of study, all those years of government service, is still not Super-scale grade. Ah! The joys of anticipation on the eve of an upgrade…the congratulatory messages from my community and my colleagues in the service… What greater happiness can any human being look forward to after three-and-a-half decades of life on earth?

As the clock on the tower of the State Secretariat Building strikes 1pm, my colleagues and I descend the spiral staircase leading to the ground floor. It's time for lunch.

The outstretched branches of the lofty rain trees provide a temporary respite from the scorching sun. We ascend another flight of stairs to the staff canteen located on the third floor. In contrast to the Mughal and Moorish architecture of the office building, the cafeteria is lodged in a modern, dull three-storey block, situated next to an open-air car park which, after office hours, metamorphoses into a badminton court. I am intrigued by the traditional exterior of the State Secretariat Building as well as the interior hierarchy among its officers, signified by the size of the dark Nyatoh desks we sit behind and the number of square feet of carpeting on the floors of each of our rooms. There's a perverse logic to our bureaucracy, where space available is in inverse proportion to space needed and bureaucratic paper has a tendency to sink to the lowest point before being dealt with. The irony here is that besides the small desk and no carpet, the lower ranks have nowhere to put their mountains of buff folders while their comfortable superiors have six metres of empty bookshelves. I correct myself, not empty; there are of course the inevitable mementos of overseas trips and overseas visitors; the red-coated beefeaters (for non-Hindu colleagues?) from London, the ceramic clogs from Holland and the miniature flags on shaky wire poles.

I am struck by how our office canteen is, at first sight, no respecter of hierarchy. Officers, clerks, secretaries and even an occasional peon or office boy mingle freely while everyone queues up to fill their plates with rice and the various accompaniments. However, when we sit down at the large rectangular or smaller square tables with the Formica tops, the demarcation begins.

We officers migrate to the farthest corner of the room to sit before a view of the angsanas and the rain trees, where it happens to be most quiet. In my corner, with my colleagues from the budget and economic divisions of the Treasury, I hold court. The other staff flock to the centre of each floor, gathering around drink vending machines as they chatter.

I choose a slice of fried tenggiri fish and sambal chicken to top my plate of rice. Sitting next to Siva, I tease him about how his plate gleams with oil from the mutton curry, as does his hair slicked down with Brylcreem.

"When I get my promotion, I can imagine my father telling his friends at the gurdwara, 'My son is no more an ordinary civil servant. He is now an extra-ordinary, senior civil servant.'"

Siva, sipping on a glass of iced Milo, looks up when I say that.

Later, other colleagues gather at the table for teh tarik and curry puffs. I launch into quizzes, riddles and jokes, a regular feature of our mealtime entertainment. My colleagues welcome this eagerly, pleased to escape momentarily from the pressure of their bosses, whom they say do nothing but stress about budgets and balance of payment deficits. I am the most talkative of them during lunch—an articulate speaker.

"Who is the only Sikh who can stay underwater forever?" I ask, looking around at everyone while rolling my eyes and twisting my moustache.

"We're drowning in your riddles, Santokh. Rescue us with your quick answer," Lim replies.

"Juswant Singh Gill... Just one, get it?" I say.

The team roars with laughter.

"Please continue," says Siva as I lean forwards and help myself to a second curry puff.

"You are most kind," I respond. "Indeed, almost as kind as my esteemed American visitor from the World Bank, who told the guard that he came to see 'the jovial gentleman in the white hat'."

My colleagues chuckle. Lim points at my white turban and laughs the loudest. "Santokh, you are a rare friend since you make jokes about yourself."

"Now supposing Sarjit Singh, Sukhdev Singh and Suret Singh take the train from Kuala Lumpur to Singh-apur, Sarjit Singh and Suret Singh got off in Seremban. How many arrive in Singh-apur?"

"Only one, Sukhdev Singh," they answer, drumming their spoons on their plates.

I beam at my audience, savouring the joy of being the maestro of this conversation. With a gesture imitative of Winston Churchill, I raise my right hand and extend my first two fingers in a V shape. Again, I relish the slight bewilderment I discern in my colleagues' eyes. I feel my voice echo around the canteen:

"T-W-O, two."

"Two; how so, Santokh?" Siva asks.

I pause, as a craftsman would. "Well, you all have overlooked Suppo Singh."

"You certainly deserve that victory sign, Santokh." Lim claps.

Although telling jokes is an art I'd polished during my school-days at the Victoria Institution and enjoy displaying now, I also consider it my duty to help my sedate civil-service colleagues relax those controlled demeanours they put on in the office. My colleagues admire my facial contortions and dramatic gestures, and have even suggested that I take part in a drama to portray a Bhangra dancer. They point me to the notice pasted on the canteen wall about the cultural-night festival to be held later that month. Food for thought, certainly.

When I return to my desk, I overhear Siva saying, "If Santokh gets his promotion, we won't see that much of him. I'd rather see more of him."

That weekend, I attend a dinner in my honour at the community club. There, at the same table, I meet again my former—and the most admired—teacher at the VI, Ganga Singh Master. As I am about to finish my plate of vegetarian samosas, I overhear a man with a golden pin on his turban say, "You mean to say this clown is going to be responsible for the most serious thing in our lives—money?"

My dessert begins to taste like the juice of neem leaves. Golden Pin's wife shakes her shawl in his face and looks over at me to stop him from gossiping. Ganga Master stands up, helping himself to more pakora. His voice, though not any louder than usual, catches all their attention. "If someone is humorous, we cannot assume he must be frivolous. Similarly, we cannot take a person seriously just because he wears a golden pin."

The guests laugh out loud and clap in approval.

Golden Pin twists open the gold crêpe paper around the ladoo and throws it onto the floor.

Despite Ganga Master's most kind defence, Golden Pin's remark still stings. There will be a dozen kirpans drawn from jealous but smiling members within our community. I will have to invest in a dagger-proof shield for my back.

"Santokh, I am so glad our community has someone of your good nature in the civil service," Ganga Master addresses me. "Incidentally, did you know that your Chief Secretary was one of my students in our alma mater?" He clasps my shoulders and shakes me.

"No, I didn't, Ganga Master."

"Poor chap; when he first joined us after his primary school in Malacca, he felt lost in my English language class. To his credit, he hung in there." Ganga Master adjusts his starched white turban. "I gave him special tuition gratis after school because I was impressed by his determination to catch up after his disadvantages in the kampung. He stayed back after school to practise his English with his urban classmates. He earned a decent credit for his efforts in his Cambridge School Certificate."

"Great man, our Chief Secretary," I say.

"He is so grateful that to this day, he never forgets to visit me or, failing that, to send a present or at least a card for every one of my birthdays. What a gem of a boss you have. If you meet him, please send him my regards and remind him how proud I am of him." Ganga Master's cheeks glow, competing with the gulab jamuns.

"Thank you, Ganga Master, I have no reason to go to see someone in such a high position as his, but if I get the honour I shall certainly send him your regards."

When I receive the news that I am to proceed immediately to England for a three-month training course, I congratulate myself; this must be preparation for my imminent elevation. On my course papers, I score A grades. I know my father's eyes will say more than the contents of my boss's letter of commendation. When the time comes to return home, I am singing songs of joy from my mother's favourite Hindi movies, thinking of the promotion that awaits me. I arrange my certificates inside a paper folder in their proper order: distinction on top, followed by outstanding and then the ordinary passes. I tuck the souvenirs and gifts between the folds of my clothes in my luggage. For my father and my wife, I bought little Big Bens; for my boss, a copper tooling of the Tower Bridge; for Lim and Siva, a Cadbury Milk Tray selection each.

When I return to work, Siva and Lim greet me with glum expressions. Lim scratches his brush-like hair and looks at Siva, who finally breaks the news. The Treasury post I had been looking forward to is going to be filled by someone from a different Ministry; a man I know. Badruddin Samad.

The news hits me hard. I look at the gifts I had brought from the UK. The image of a miniature Union Jack on the plastic bag stares back at me. I drop the bag onto the last rack of a filing cabinet. The copper tooling hits the hollow bottom of the drawer with a loud clang. "That Bad Sam has cheated me of my upgrading. Was I sent on a course to be put out of the way?" Kicking the drawer shut is hardly enough for me to vent my frustration, so I bang my fists on its steel top. Siva and Lim avert their eyes. I step away from my desk and ask them, "Why must I be left 'acting' in my present post? Am I a professional actor?"

Lim tries to persuade me to calm down.

"I have been swindled. Samad is the nephew of our Permanent Secretary. We used to tease him that he was the Man from UNCLE but now the joke is on me." Siva nods in sympathetic agreement. My two buddies tell me how upset they were when they first heard the sad news. They suggest I write an appeal.

I find myself writing a two-page letter, with the approval of my boss at the Treasury, to the Director General of the Public Service Department.

A week later, as I am about to leave my desk for lunch, I receive a reply that my appeal has been rejected. By then, my spirits are so low that I can hardly squash the letter up. At the canteen table, I shred one roti canai after another into pieces before pouring ladles of spicy fish curry over my plate. Piercing pieces of roti canai with a fork, putting them into my mouth, I can't taste a thing.

"Santokh, could it be that some of your jokes about various communities were considered bureaucratically incorrect by some officers in the Public Service Department?" Siva asks.

"I never meant to offend anyone with my jokes," I reply.

I overhear Siva's whisper to Lim that there will surely be a sharp drop thereafter in the number of jokes from me. I tell them that as a Treasury officer, I am accustomed to sending rejection letters not receiving them.

I consult Nizam, the Secretary to the Promotions and Appeals Board. He was also my second residential-college roommate at the University of Malaya. He advises me that Tan Sri Abdullah is well known for his capacity for kasihan: sympathy for others. A number of times, he has heard that Tan Sri Abdullah personally intervened to approve appeals for transfers of staff so that staff members could serve in the same towns as their spouses.

Early the next morning, I steamroll into the office of the Chief Secretary to the Government, the head of the entire civil service. I ask his secretary if I can see him most urgently about a very important matter. After checking with his boss, the secretary says I can see him now.

"Sir, I have been robbed."

"Robbed…?" Tan Sri looks at me over the spectacles resting on his cheeks.

"Yes, Tan Sri, what is supposed to be mine has been snatched from me."

"Sorry to hear that."

"It is my promotion I have been robbed of, sir." I stand upright in front of the carved teak desk to present my case, without my usual humour but at least with great conviction. But Tan Sri Abdullah is glancing at the clock on the wall. I have to change tack. It's now or never.

I tuck errant strands of hair back into my white turban with my mother's multipurpose four-millimetre short knitting needle. "Above all, sir, if I don't get this promotion, I shall have to leave town after applying for a transfer to the remotest district in the East Coast. I shall become the laughing stock of the Sikh community."

"Oh. Why is that?" Tan Sri Abdullah sits up. "What have they got to do with this?"

"They have already given me a lavish subscription dinner to celebrate my sure promotion. The boxes overflowing with jalebi and the payda wrapped up in saffron and red strings are just examples of the extravagance at the party thrown in my honour, sir."

"Your Treasury won't allow that for official parties."

"Never, sir. I worry some may even ask for a refund of their subscriptions for the dinner. How to face them again, sir?"

Now that I have the Chief's full attention, I deliver my pukka line as casually as I can. "By the way, sir… I met my uncle, Ganga Master, at the party. I believe you know him."

Tan Sri blinks, and then his face turns red. "He is your uncle? Oh, I didn't know that. I am very fond of him and hold him in high regard. He was my favourite English master. I had no idea he is your uncle. How strange he has never mentioned it before. He really is your uncle?"

"Yes, both you and I were his star students." I raise my right hand in the air.

"Ha, that is wonderful that you are not only his nephew, but also his protégé. Did he tell you anything else about me?"

"Yes, Tan Sri, he told me how proud he was of you and to send you his regards."

Tan Sri looks jubilant. "I do so wish to see him again soon." His eyes even get moist.

"He has gone back to his ancestral home in Punjab after his retirement."

His face drops. "I'm so sorry that I won't be able to see him again."

Tan Sri Abdullah promises me before I leave the room that as Chairman of the Promotions Board he will consider my appeal. I am so pleased that I decide to treat Nizam, Siva and Lim to chicken and mutton briyani at Bilal Restaurant later that evening.

Nizam whispers to me that the Board is swamped and unable to hold its regular meetings. Therefore, my appeal will go straight to the Tan Sri for the final decision. He says that if I stand at the thin rear-exit door of the dining room while they have lunch, I can eavesdrop on their conversation.

Thus, I find myself listening in during lunch the next day on the sounds of cutlery and Nizam saying, "Here is the appeal from Santokh Singh of the Treasury."

"Yes, the nephew of my ex-VI teacher, Ganga Master..." Tan Sri's reply gives me a tingle down my spine.

"He is a hardworking officer, Tan Sri," Nizam says.

"I am remembering my schooldays. Terrible times in some ways, but necessary. Ganga Master, big, terrifying but helpful. He reminds me so vividly of my English lessons. He beat out *The Rime of the Ancient Mariner* with the familiarity of a chapatti maker, one palm slapping the other, as he chanted in sing-song gusto." Tan Sri Abdullah's voice grows louder.

It is an ancient Mariner,
And he stoppeth one of three.
"By thy long grey beard and glittering eye,
Now wherefore stopp'st thou me?

Tan Sri is in full steam. "Ganga Master who made us learn the whole of Coleridge's poem by heart.

"Ganga Master, his pure-white turban bobbing up and down in time with the verse.

"Ganga Master, who personally tutored me after my Special Malay Class when I stumbled through my English grammar on the past perfect progressive at the age of thirteen.

"Ganga Master, who glowed with pride when he saw the creditable Credit appear on my academic record.

"Ganga Master's white turban; Santokh's white turban..."

It is wonderful hearing my name recited next to Ganga Master's.

"I rarely overrule the PSD on service matters, but this time I have to make an exception. I cannot allow one of my officers to be humiliated in front of his own community. Kasihan dia. I empathise with him. After all, accommodating all communities, including minorities, is another unique Malaysian feature, like our rojak. And Santokh has very good confidential reports from his Treasury bosses."

This final justification sets the seal on Tan Sri's decision. Promotion it is. I wonder very briefly what will happen to Badruddin.

Days later, the peon places my mail on my table. The glitter of pink and gold on envelope edges sticks out from that pile. By the time I come to the fifth wedding invitation, my hands grow weary, so I insert the letter opener back into its case. I throw the invitations into my wastepaper basket. As I dust off shimmering flakes, I spy a medium-sized brown envelope stamped, "Sulit/ Confidential". Just like my promotion letter to be beneath these other envelopes. The letter is from the Director General of the Public Service Department, congratulating me on my promotion.

I'm embarrassed as I see Lim wipe his palm on his pants after he shakes my hand to congratulate me. My palms are soaked in sweat on reading this letter, even after I dab them on both sides of my turban. Now that desire has become fact, doubts set in. Will I end up a victim like the one Ganga Master used to quote to us from Goethe—"Beware of what you wish for in youth lest you achieve it in middle life"? I think of all those wedding invitations with the expectation of a Super-scale present to the happy couple from their Super-scale guest. I am ashamed I guffawed when bank officers at the gurdwara grumbled about the problems of promotion being like balancing a chapatti griddle on their turbans. Must I now give up my carefree time with my badminton and hockey buddies? Am I ready to pay the full price of this promotion? Was I too eager for promotion when it seemed I could have it? Too eager for respect from my community, caught up with losing face if the promotion were not mine? Had I really forgotten the obligations that come with elevated status when I tossed out all those invitations? How will I live down my big lie about Ganga Master being my real uncle? Had I lost sight of the devastation my new status is going to wreak on my precious wallet and now on my guilty soul? Now that I've got my promotion, will I have to move without leaving any forwarding address? This seems to be my mid-life crisis come early, and I am not yet middle-aged.

I call Nizam. "Which Sikh has a teardrop from the corner of each eye? One small joy at being promoted, another larger regret for the financial demands of his community."

"Santokh?"

"You bet!"

Later that night, I think over the events of the day. True, the government has given me what I have worked so hard for, but it came to me only after I had made an appeal in which I lied. Is this how a promotion comes to me? As I turn this over and over in my mind, I find that like Macbeth, I have murdered sleep for the night. When I finally drop off, not before a good few cockerels have sounded, I see my father standing over me with his leather belt, hissing, "My son, the liar, what will you become next? A murderer..."

The bite from the brass buckle makes my skin swell. I look down at where the belt scored my thigh and see two bright green eyes staring up at me; the tiger's teeth press painfully into my leg. With my father's voice, the tiger addresses me, "What? Are you a child in Standard 3 to lie from pride and fear? No, not the Ganga Master's nephew, nor are you my son."

I am awake after a broken hour's rest and covered in perspiration. I don't touch the mug of tea which my wife made for me, stirred with fresh cow's milk and a dash of ginger powder.

By the time the magpie-robins sing their wake-up call, I have drafted in my mind a letter to Tan Sri Abdullah. I fold a half-inch margin on the right and left sides of a letter-pad page before drawing up my pen from the ink bottle, remembering how to my father it was never "Quink", always "Quick".

Y Bhg Tan Sri Abdullah

Chief Secretary to the Government

I am deeply grateful for your kindest intervention to offer me a promotion to Super-scale grade.

Although this was my dream, now that it has finally happened to me, it is confusing me.

I have a confession to make. I'm neither Ganga Master's nephew nor his star pupil.

Like most good Asians I call him "Uncle" as a term of respect. I was not his special protégé either. To cover up, I misled you that Ganga Master had retired to Punjab.

On the other hand, Tan Sri, as the Head of the entire civil service you are like a Government Uncle to me. If you say it's all right for me to accept, then I must. As Asians, if anyone asks or tells us twice, we should submit.

I trust your reputation for compassion, sir.

I remain, with all due respect, sir,

Yours humbly,
Santokh Singh

I take my letter to Tan Sri's secretary and ask him if he can show it to Tan Sri immediately.

I also send a copy of my letter to Nizam.

He phones me two days later. "It was the Victoria Institution Old Boys' Dinner last night, you know." I hear his voice slow to a drawl. "Tan Sri told me this morning how much he enjoyed it. He sat next to Ganga Master. He tells me that he and Ganga Master had a long chat about family and outstanding pupils. And about a confession which worked in your favour."

NAMING NAMES

Kandiah was one in a million.

Fine.

Certainly at least one in a thousand, if one wanted to be fastidious about place values. His father had bestowed upon him the same name that a few hundred other sires had granted their offspring.

This proliferation of Kandiahs, Kandayahs, Kandasamys, Kanagalingams, Kanagaratnams, Kanagasabais, Kanagupeiars and many other names was to become the source of much creative activity within the Malayan Jaffna Tamil community throughout the centuries. You could not utter any one of these names, let alone complete a sentence about the namesake, without half a dozen members of the community pouncing on you with "Which Kandiah?" or "Whose Kanagaratnam? Sinnappu's son? Pariappu's nephew or Sinappah's drunken son-in-law?" If your listener wanted to be helpful, a temptation which was rarely resisted, he would volunteer with "You mean Railways Kandiah?" If said gentleman had retired, he might say, "You must be meaning PWD Kandiah." If said person were still active as a builder of roads, he might say, "JKR Kandiah." Such voluntary assistance in identifying the right Kandiah was always inadequate. There was more than one JKR Kandiah and half a dozen PWD Kandiahs on the loose.

Since these Kandiahs were mere civilians, numerology was of no help. People carried their identity cards with them, but it was enough trouble remembering one's own. "So, do you mean Kandiah Identity Card No. 3318840, Kandiah Identity Card No. 8813340 or the Kandiah 4418830?" Do you see how that is unhelpful?

Citing surnames together with their given names—"You mean Kandiah Bottomley or Kandiah Topmann?"—could have stood out and helped, but the community was not accustomed to using these. There were no surnames to live up to or to live down. The historian's alternative of, "It was Kandiah the Eighth, who had only one wife all his life; Kandiah the Ninth, who had none; and Kandiah the Fifth, who had never led his country into battle" was hardly useful as there were just too many Houses of Kandiah.

If the historian offered no guidance in discriminating within the world of Kandiahs, the geographer fared no better. "You mean Kandiah of the Valley?" or "You must be meaning Riverside Kandiah" was just a bit closer to a solution since most of the Kandiahs were found huddled in towns, indistinguishable by contour or compass. Indeed, no academic or educator had offered an Alexandrian solution to the Gordian knot of Kandiahs. Kandiahs were both major and minor, and since there were as many in class 5D now as there had been in 5A then, ranks and levels did not advance the subject any further.

However, these outsider problems were rarely understood by members of the Tribe of Kandiah themselves.

"Which stupid fool cannot tell the difference between a King Kandiah and the garden variety?" asked a Kandiah who claimed to have strangled a python or two in his youth.

"How can you compare an original Mona Lisa with a small postcard Mona Lisa sold on the roadside?" snorted another pioneering Kandiah, whose acquaintance with art was at an even more primitive stage. The only artists he had been introduced to by his British expatriate teacher were Constable and Turner. He could not say for certain which one of them was responsible for the Mona Lisa.

"You mean an original 'Made in England Kandiah' should stay in the same room as a local product?" As rooms now were only a fraction as large as those in the old PWD government quarters, the indignities were enhanced.

Needless to say, this attitude hardly satisfied the wider non-Kandiah community and there was no shortage of comment and suggestions for solutions.

"If the Americans and the Russians can have a treaty for the non-proliferation of nuclear weapons, why can't we have one for the non-proliferation of Kandiahs?" queried one of the community's many international-affairs specialists. "How can we rely on these small boys to handle such a highly sophisticated name without getting into trouble?" A proposal which gained considerable support suggested putting each Kandiah into a time bracket tagged with a significant event.

"These journalist Kandiahs think only of today. My son was born before the Japanese had even heard of Pearl Harbor, Emerald Harbour or any other jewel harbour."

From which Kandiah, the controversy extended to which war and even which point of said war. No sooner had the Kandiahs drawn the line for their war babies born at the end of the Second World War, leaving the Korean-boom offspring out, than another cluster of Kandiahs blanked out any heirs born after Pearl Harbor.

"A law should be passed to say that anyone who was named Kandiah after the War should be renamed with a lesser name."

"Any Kandiah born after World War I should be banished from this country to make his name elsewhere—not just rest on his father's laurels."

Prof. Kandiah from the University of Malaya did his usual erudite summing up, "This whole mess comes from too much freedom. How else can you explain this free-for-all, this chaos where the riff-raff can grab names from our illustrious families—and in broad daylight too? There is nothing a man can call his own. Not even the name his own father gave him. If a thief picks your pocket, he can be arrested. If he counterfeits money, he can be jailed. If he sells imitation goods, his shop gets raided. The state and the law are extremely good at catching small boys; all the more so with giving out parking tickets. However, anyone is free to plunder, murder and rape our names. What we need is a central planning committee for the naming of names. That may be radical for our Parkinson's law committees that specialise in trivia like GNP, GDP and Gee, Gee, Gee. At least, a registrar of individual names is an absolute necessity. Imagine the chaos to our free-enterprise system if every corner shop called itself General Motors and any scoundrel could set up a bank and name itself the Bank of England."

Lawyer Kandiah from Shearn, Shook and Skrine snorted, "Vat is all this vailing about, ah? Imitation is the highest form of flattery. The more Kandiahs there are, the greater the tribute to the original Kandiah. Can a roadside artist sell as many reprints as Picasso? The more the merrier. Some of my Chinese friends kill themselves and their wives in the process to make sure they produce a son to carry on the family surname. We are getting Kandiahs not just at cheap sale prices but for free. And not just while stocks last but in perpetuity. Kandiahs of the world go forth; multiply. Don't be divided by doubt and dissent. As in the insurance business, your target for this month should be a million. Surely we can do better than the humble rabbit with just his carrots."

"Very clever, my mass-produced Kandiahs. How does one tell between Kandiah the Distinguished and Kandiah the Dumb? Which is Hamlet and which is the drain sweeper of Denmark?"

The community descended into darkness. Did Kandiah X equal Kandiah Y? Wasn't Kandiah P worth at least two of Kandiah Q?

From this pitch-black night, a light flickered. A seventy-year-old Kandiah stumbled on a means of distinguishing between himself and another Kandiah in the same queue to collect their monthly pension at the local post office. He had discovered a means of defusing the confusion in their community.

"It is the greatest thing since the splitting of the atom. No, no, none of this false modesty. I have never been one for any kind of falsehood. It is even greater than Alexander the Great's cutting of the Gordian knot. Our community shall be free. Free of confusion, chaos and calamity. Did you notice, the other Kandiah keeps hunching all the time, his eyes always drooping in the direction of his stomach? Eureka Kandiah, the answer to our dilemma, our quo vadis is before our very eyes. The nickname."

"Hereafter, that Kandiah queuing in front of me shall be Vaithu Vali Kandiah—Stomach Ache Kandiah."

A thousand flowers bloomed. And this time the decimal was slightly nearer to the right place.

From apparent ailments, the nicknames spread to portions of the anatomy. There was Kundi Kandiah or Backside Kandiah, who was the butt of misleading jokes which suggested that he was a buttock pincher. At the bottom of it all was a more innocent premise: this Kandiah used to amble like a matron. In the process, he gave no little prominence to his posterior. So in addition to history and geography there was a personal distinguishing mark. The sobriquets were hardly confined to ailments and postures.

There was Kandiah who gave lifts in his jalopy. That would be putting it mildly. He would not merely offer a lift but insist on one. Not just to friends or mere acquaintances but to just about any passer-by. There were no complaints about his driving or the nature of the conversations he struck with his passengers. His nickname arose from what he was in the habit of doing when his grateful and innocent passenger was about to alight from his vehicle. This Kandiah would clear his throat and announce the fare that he expected.

That was Tax–i Kandiah.

A Kandiah with different transport needs was in the habit of loitering at bus stops. The furthest thing from his mind, however, was a bus. He lay there in ambush for any slight acquaintance whose car had to slow down at bus stops and leapt in since there were few separate lanes for buses. On the surface of it, he would be a ripe candidate for the title of Bus Stop Kandiah. But that was not to be. His cutting down on, or rather eliminating, bus fares from his budget was merely the last lap before he stepped out from the shadow of the bus stop to acquire his very own car. The number of streets with separate bus lanes and bus stops began to increase.

Own Car Kandiah never looked back. He merely turned down numerous offers of lifts from his old acquaintances and his new ones with a "No appu. I've got my own car."

A variation on this game of musical cars was played by another Kandiah. His affliction was that he owned one car too many. His flourishing legal practice and his clients' penchant for sending him to exotic places overseas with their files and their money were the road to his troubles. He rode off in a different car each time and was late for his appointments most mornings because after deciding which tie to wear, he had little energy left for the crucial decision of which car to take off in.

Multi Car Kandiah won friends and influenced people neither through a Dale Carnegie course nor through his winning smile. He would make strategic requests for lifts from potential ring-leaders of the community, who lived to tell their grandchildren,

"With all his limousines, Multi Car Kandiah still preferred to ride in my car."

Lest it be concluded that transport, cars and lifts had wiped out women, wine and song from the community, we shall turn to other Kandiahs whose travelling habits were more nondescript. They were given to joyous singing in all sorts of places, including some very unlikely ones: funerals, for instance. After much wailing and screaming, the womenfolk would allow the menfolk to leave their households, bringing the bodies of the departed for cremation. At those otherwise thoroughly dreary occasions, these Kandiahs would burst into song. As they were religious songs, no frivolity was implied. But it did not stand in the way of a veritable talent time as other Kandiahs would burst into melody. One Kandiah would organise trips and picnics to seaside resorts for pensioners and widows with only one object in mind—song. More than one nickname was composed from all this music. There was Paatter Kara Kandiah or Song Man Kandiah, Talent Time Kandiah and just plain M. Kandiah—M for the music he would hum—while M for money was on the minds of most of his fellow men.

There was also another Kandiah who got his nickname from his relationship with the birds. This was with a certain bird. Unfortunately, not the "bird" which in English can refer to a woman but, literally, the feathered one. This Kandiah sang a "song of sixpence" while in primary school although our currency was in dollars and cents. He never thought that as in the nursery rhyme, where the maiden's nose was pecked by a blackbird, his ear would one day be pecked by a crow in Jaffna.

That was Kahang Kothi Kandiah or Crow Pecked Kandiah.

While five-year plans and family plans were the "in" thing, another Kandiah believed in letting nature take its course. As with the case of inflation, the number of his children had to be expressed in double digits that would shame some rabbits and many a Roman Catholic. Asian grandmothers and mothers-in-law were supposed to bask in the glory of the number of grandchildren they possessed. That was not to be for our proliferating Kandiah.

"What is this Kandiah? Like a dog you are!" the mother-in-law would reprimand each time Mrs Kandiah returned with yet another baby Kandiah. Dogs were considered of a lower social order than rabbits. She was therefore more concerned with conveying her low regard for such behaviour than with the accuracy of the analogy from the animal kingdom. The reprimands did not prove adequate. Having breached the two-digit barrier, he galloped past family six-a-side cricket, full soccer and then even rugby teams.

That was 19 Children Kandiah. Rumour had it that like the Group of 77 in the United Nations, the actual number exceeded this particular mile- and millstone that hung around his neck.

The energies of the Kandiahs were not all of the 19-children variety. Many of them were noted for their civic consciousness, which was expressed in many forms.

One of them spent much of his energy on keeping a particular society alive. This society had an unusual purpose in which it linked the next world with the present one. It focused entirely on that point in time when souls departed from their bodies.

Financial aid was available to the widows and orphans of departed members. This was provided within hours of their departure without numerous forms filled in triplicate, followed by equally numerous reminders sent in duplicates. To take care of the funeral expenses and immediate departures the society collected a very modest sum of one dollar payable every month in cash. IOUs, credit cards and other forms of non-cash or delayed payments of the monthly subscription were not permitted, thanks to a single device. The most important office bearer in the society, namely the Treasurer, would turn up without fail every month at the homes of members, with even fewer words than President Coolidge could muster. For this very first visit even, this Kandiah had only two words on his lips: "One dollar?" For all subsequent visits his telegraphic style improved even further with just "One?"

So mesmerising were those words, or rather this particular word, that the benevolent organisation surpassed the record of the World Bank and other financial organisations with AAA credit ratings. There was not a single delayed payment, let alone a default, in the history of the society's existence.

As this Kandiah rode, or rather walked, away into the sunset after making the society's payments to the stricken widow, many an orphan was heard to ask, "Who was that unmasked man who just gave us all this money and left before we could thank him, without so much as a 'Hi Yo Silver' or 'Kemo Sabe' from his Tonto?" That was the work of Oru Velli Kandiah (i.e., One Dollar Kandiah).

Another civic-conscious Kandiah did not merely get involved; he got immersed totally in this favourite American pursuit of happiness and security. The slight variation was that it was not for him but for others. He was Honorary Secretary of countless associations ranging from his school's Old Boys' Association to the Boy Scouts and the Cricket Council to the Spastic Children's Association. One of the more than seven parts he played in his lifetime was that of Honorary Secretary of the local housing area's Residents' Association. So vigilant a guardian was he of the security of all households in his flock that they had little need for burglar alarms, security guards or Alsatians. In this capacity, his favourite story was that of the senior army officer's house, which had been broken into in the early hours of the morning while the officer was away. The wife could hear the "eight footsteps of the four burglars creeping up the staircase". She screamed for help.

"She could have called for the Police, called for the Army, yelled for Securicor, Safeguards, the Home Guard, her neighbours or just hollered for help to the 300-large neighbourhood. Instead, her first SOS was for Kandiah!" he beamed.

That was Take Care Kandiah, who took care of everyone else before himself.

Lest this turn into a census enumeration of all the Kandiahs—illustrious and otherwise—we shall wind this tale up with just one other Kandiah. He was the one whose creativity went beyond the trivia on birth certificates and passports when he went around giving nicknames to all the other Kandiahs. That was Funny Names Kandiah.

It was this Kandiah who told me this story.

HIS MOTHER'S JOY

I am the happiest mother of all mothers.

That's why I am treating my neighbour Mrs Chong to my sweetest traditional delicacies. After my 6am ritual dipper bath I apply talcum powder to my face and my usual red pottu. I tighten my hair bun before I place the oil lamps around Lord Ganesha's statue in the pooja room. I sing Vathapi Ganapatim to thank Lord Ganesha for blessing my son.

"I know how you love dumplings, Mrs Chong!" I raise a Pyrex bowl to her.

The gula Melaka syrup oozing down our wrists from my sweet kolukattai signals the best part of our mighty mid-morning tea.

"What is the good news ah?" She takes "last bites" of many dumplings.

"A Malaysian Civil Service Officer. How many mothers can celebrate the awarding of an MCS-ship to their own son? This very select group are the ice cream of all ice creams, cream lah lah cream or something Frenchified. Why are they called Mandarins? Many of them don't speak Mandarin, hai, moh?"

"Mr Chong and I can what." She swings her palm, which seems more like her scooping the aroma of my food towards her nose.

I join her laughing as I pour her a second cup of her favourite hot black coffee with three teaspoons of white sugar.

"The other Chinese there talk chop, chop in Cantonese or Hokkienese. All of them talk in legalese. The officers come in light brown, yellow, chocolate and some in white but none is orange. But mandarin or tangerine, they are, as we say, the durian of our eyes and of our tongues. In the bad old British colonial days, Siva's father said, our own leaders complained that the MCS was neither Malayan nor civil and didn't provide much service to us."

"Now, how different?" Mrs Chong asks.

"Our sons are shining and so are our stars. Siva's father started work as a junior clerk with a Junior Cambridge Certificate. After thirty-five years he was promoted to Office Assistant, the chief of all the chief clerks, and was awarded an MBE by the British Colonial High Commissioner, Sir Henry Gurney. He has a moustache. As OA, he was just a whisker below MCS officers in rank. He knew many more details than they but he belonged to a different class. When Siva first wrote the alphabet with his forefinger on the tray of auspicious raw rice grains before starting primary school, we knew he would harvest a University degree. My honours-graduate son is now starting not merely one rung above where his father finished his lifelong career, but one entire ladder above him. His father is my hero, but Siva should be everyone's superhero."

"My mother also treat my brother like her boss." Mrs Chong peers up from looking through our album. I point at Siva in his graduation gown with me smiling more than him in the photograph.

"Right from kindergarten, I went through every line of his schoolwork and later his homework from school with him, a hot mug of Horlicks or Ovaltine beside him."

"Your son, so lucky ah."

"I am taking camphor and coconuts to offer a special pooja at our temple to Lord Siva before Friday prayers. When my

son was little, he played snakes and ladders all over our govern-
ment-quarters neighbourhood. Next, he will play ladders upon
ladders with the top civil servants. What happened to the snakes,
Mrs Chong?"

I lift the tudung saji for Mrs Chong's next dumpling.

"Mrs Kandiah, I know a civil serpent born in the year of the
golden snake. One day he hopes to be the king cobra of his department. 'Every snake will have his year,' he claims. I must finish my
household chorus before my husband returns. Otherwise, he will
accuse me of playing mah-jong all day. He says that if I do good
housekeeping, then he will be a good housewife keeper for me."

"Chorus? So you sing while you work? I too have to hurry, Mrs
Chong. I must withdraw my money before the post office closes."

Clutching my black umbrella, I usually wait for the chicaks
on the ceiling to stop their inauspicious clicking, my signal to
depart. However, this afternoon, I didn't wait for them to be
quiet. The magpie-robins in white and black, the black-naped
"golden" orioles, the yellow-vented bulbuls and mynahs whistle
in my garden. It resembles the one we had at our former government quarters in Scott Road, shaded by coconut, banana
and papaya trees, further edged with bougainvillea, hibiscus and
orchid plants. I have my own mango tree on the lawn in Thamby
Abdullah Road, still within Brickfields, where Siva's father built a
bungalow for us after his retirement.

"You all are also celebrating my son's appointment ah?" I tease
them, strewing seeds and grains. "May Lord Siva bless you. Siva
and his father are too busy to feed you birds."

The post office is packed. Those on the way out were recycling
discarded government stationery for cleaning their thumbs, black

from the multi-thumb-printing needed on government forms. As I queue for "incoming mail", as I call it, a lady with a headscarf returns my smile.

Although I have convinced my neighbour, Mrs Chong, my greater challenge is to prove to this strange but gentle kitten that I am the most devoted mother any son can have. The more people I can persuade about my hopes and dreams for Siva, the more likely they will become true. I crease the pleats in my saree, ready for my battle.

"Makcik, my treasure from the MCS has just been posted to the Treasury. Now he can be my treasurer and demand a doctor's ransom, I mean dowry, for a fair graduate bride from his future parents-in-law. We ordinary people understand a few ringgit and sen. He deals in millions."

I love seeing her nod. "At his birth, his horoscope predicted all this exactly. If your friends or relatives in the government are applying for a car or a housing loan, inform me. My son can put in the magic word to his colleagues. What are these tiny loans compared to the millions that heads of government departments humbly seek the Treasury's blessings to spend?"

She nods again. "The Treasury is *the* Ministry of Finance. The director general for income tax, the accountant general, the biggest civilian generals all come under this Ministry."

"Yes, so I heard." Her smile shows me she can't wait to share my news with everyone.

I should finish my story with this mild lady before the postal clerk calls me.

"Of all the government departments, their staff start work the earliest and they are the last to leave their offices. Every single thing they do is on 'His Majesty's Service'. When they sneeze, the whole government gets pneumonia, including those in the Ministry of Health! Yet, they end their letters with 'I am your most obedient servant'." They have a hundred reasons for being proud yet they are sooh humble. Isn't that funny? He deals with the World Bank, the grandfather of all banks."

"What is your influential son's name?" The increasingly wide-eyed kitten, holding on to her headscarf, asks me.

"Siva, after our Lord Siva, the most powerful of all our gods. Since he was posted to the Treasury, he is our homemade Lord Siva with almost as much power as our God. Many people say 'God willing' before they promise to do anything but in the government they are more specific. They say, 'Treasury willing'."

"I must tell my husband about your son."

"Not just your husband, your family, relatives, friends and neighbours. We must share such influential persons with everyone." I wave so fast that I must seem to her as many-handed as Lord Siva himself.

Weeks later, one Sunday morning, I am at the wet market with Siva. He tiptoes along with me through the slushy floors while our nostrils, flaring then pinching, adjust to the fragrance of jasmine flowers in garlands and the less pleasing smell of raw crab, fish, prawns and squid. From a distance, I spot that same makcik in a red scarf at the chicken seller's stall.

"Son, that's the gentle lady I met at the post office last month! She was smiling to herself while I was talking to her. She must be so contented."

"I recognise her too."

"Did you meet her at the post office as well?"

"No, Amma, at the Treasury."

"What was she doing there?"

"Seeing her husband."

"Her husband? What was his business at the Treasury?"

"He works there."

"Oh, as what?"

"My immediate boss is the Principal Assistant Secretary. His superior is the Deputy Under-Secretary who reports to the Under-Secretary who then reports to the Deputy Secretary General. His chief is the No. 1 civil servant of the Treasury. That biggest of bosses is the Secretary General to the Treasury, your makcik's husband."

Siva's words pierce my eardrums. My face feels cold. The chickens' cackling grows louder. Another throat is seized and slit; blood squirts down its headless body.

"Ayoyo en Kadavulai, oh my God, the market's too crowded today. Let's go home and come back on any other day except today." I grab Siva's wrist.

As I am leaving, Puan Sri Salmah happens to look up and catch my eye. She approaches me. Siva greets her and takes the empty basket from my hand before walking opposite to talk to his friend Santokh at a vegetable stall. I am alone.

"Puan Sri, the other day at the post office, I was just joking about my little boy." I turn around looking for Siva. When I face her again, she nods.

"You know how we mothers are," I plead, ready to flee the market. Slush smudges my saree border, damp and cold, while I look again beyond the crowd for my Siva.

Puan Sri Salmah is in front of me, adjusting her scarf, releasing two curls on each side of her forehead.

"I know. My mother-in-law always boasting about her son. I think she is a joker also. My son is sure to be Prime Minister one day. She doesn't know how to be a typical grandmother. I listen and make 'donno'. Simply pretend and agree with her. She thinks I am the same kuching kurap she and my husband first met. I just act simple. I am the only Puan Sri who goes to the post office, to the market, to everywhere. Other Puan Sri never go here and there. Let people think I am just an ulu woman. That's how I meet all kinds of people. Let other people talk much first. Show off last best lah."

I watch her walking away and try not to sulk. Siva joins me, swinging the market basket, saying he wasn't sure what I needed. He asks me if I'm feeling all right, since I've suddenly turned as pale as the talcum powder on my face.

"Nothing wrong, my son, just that it's hot in that corner where you made me wait. You must take me home."

He winds down the car windows, watching me wipe my face. I turn to him, forcing a smile. "Siva, my idea is that it's about time your future mother- and father-in-law should know about your powerful new post."

Reaching home, I stagger to my kitchen headquarters. Pulling myself up among my row of spice bottles, my recycled Horlicks bottles of various sizes and my cutlery all made in "Swee-den", I call out to Mrs Chong over our fence, "I should have waited for the chicaks' silent signal before leaving the house."

"What happened to you?"

"At the chicken stall, I was the bird whose feathers were plucked out. My post-office kitten turned into a woman-eating tiger."

"Why you rubbing your forehead like that?" Mrs Chong asks.

"I am thinking of when my Siva thanks me without his usual grumbling, 'Amma, I'm embarrassed by your boasting about me'."

"What to do? Children can be ungrateful nowadays."

"So can neighbours, like my Mrs Chelliah. I'm no longer the happiest mother. But I can be the grandest grandmother we know. That post is fully vacant."

"I can't say, Mrs Kandiah, since I lost my son, my first and only child. I'm childless but my 3A-old grandnephew is the smartest dragon in the East." Mrs Chong's nostrils flare as she perks up.

"3A?"

"Last year, he was three years old. Next year, five. So this year must be 3A."

"Even his age has an A in it. He must be an all As pupil."

"If not, his parents will cane him."

"Mrs Chong, my Siva's son will become president of the World Bank one day. Will he appreciate me even less, like his father? I'll still go to the post office personally. But to such dangerous places as the market where slaughterers and tigers may prowl, I'll send his maid."

THE BAREFOOT MAN
FROM MALAYA

KARAI NAGAR, CEYLON

Rasamah's celebration of Lord Ganesha's birthday started off with an unorthodox visitation. She was taken aback by the apparition of a man standing on her front lawn, a set of fountain pens neatly clipped to the pocket of the knee-length white cotton shirt he wore over a veshti. Rasamah had been rushing to make kolukattai before her Amma woke up, when the surprised neigh of her horse outside brought her dashing to the front door. The man introduced himself as Kandasamy and asked if he might come in to have a word with her in private. This was most unusual, as such a request from a young man of a young lady he did not know, whom he had just met, breached propriety. His hair was tousled, cut in a style that suggested he wasn't from the neighbourhood. Who was he and what did he want?

"Cowherds and gardeners come through the back garden." She pointed to the grassy lane where her family's domestics entered.

"I beg your pardon. I am neither cowherd nor gardener." The visitor flipped the long white cloth over his shoulder and faced her on her own front lawn.

"We can talk out here."

"It's private. Better inside, please."

"Only if you keep it very short." Curiosity got the better of Rasamah, even as she reluctantly stepped aside to let this barefoot man in while noticing every single gesture he made, especially the way he looked at her. Rasamah waited as Kandasamy looked around at the décor. Warnings echoed in her head: her mother's, in Tamil, about the behaviour of unmarried girls, and Mother Superior's stern Irish voice when she chastised Rasamah in the convent, "Your rashness will get you into trouble."

"It's true what people have said about you. I am in great admiration of the decoration here."

"Since you care so much about people's opinions, what will they say about your visiting me while I am alone? What about my reputation now?"

"I admit my method is abrupt but my intentions are most honourable."

The embroidered curtains fluttered in the wind. The man walked to a silver vase and bent down to inhale the fragrance of jasmine tucked into the red hibiscus flowers that Rasamah had picked. He touched the feet of a miniature statue of Lord Ganesha that stood on a nearby stool. Noting this gesture of reverence, Rasamah softened a bit.

"Today...is a most auspicious day," he said.

"I know it's Vinayaka Chaturthi. That's why I am making Lord Ganesha's favourite—kolukattai." Rasamah picked up a round pillow from the floor. "But you didn't come all the way to tell me that?" She sat facing the staircase leading to Amma's bedroom.

After a few moments, Kandasamy turned his gaze directly upon her.

"I shall come to the point immediately. I was just wondering whether you would marry me."

Pin-drop silence. Rasamah pulled back, dropping the cushion from her lap in a fluster. Had she heard right? Her heart started thumping. She lowered her gaze too, because how could she look at him? The hem of her lemon-yellow skirt quivered over her ankles, paler than the glow from her oval face.

"Excuse me, but what did you say?"

"I asked if you would marry me."

Rasamah stole a look at this brazen man who had just wandered into her house to make her an outrageous proposition. She felt a hot flush rise up her cheeks and pressed her palms to them, as if that would make words come.

"What a shocking question. No one has ever dared to…to ask me this before."

She gestured for him to sit.

"I regret I don't have the time to follow tradition right now." Kandasamy took a seat, but no one had ever dared to lean quite so nonchalantly in a seat in her home before.

It made Rasamah feel both different and doubtful. "What do you mean?"

"No dowry for me." There he sat, looking at her intently, the serious purpose clear in his gaze.

"I beg your pardon?" Rasamah pursed her lips, thinking.

"I mean it."

An uncomfortable stillness reigned in the room.

"You've proposed directly to a girl, alone, without going through her parents, all her aunties and some uncles." She spoke without looking at him, drawing imaginary designs on the hand-loomed rug with her large toe. "You're trying to put these elders out of their matchmaking business."

Kandasamy pulled out a small notebook from his pocket, opening it to where a red ribbon marked the page. "To be able to marry," he read, "one must check wealth, traditional learning—including astrology and poetry—English education, employment, village origin…"

Rasamah waved her hands to stop him mid-recital. "If you can ignore my family and talk marriage to me directly, what makes you think I should concern myself with your long list from your little notebook?" The unorthodox meeting was making her perspire, and she felt out of breath.

"Fine. What I want to know is, what do you say to my proposal?" He lowered his shoulders, going down on one knee.

"Please get up. Sit, please."

Rasamah could hear in the background the movement and voices of the maids along the lounge. She clutched her hands fearing the conclusions they would draw upon seeing a stranger, a man at that, kneeling down before her. Her head began to spin.

Then he sat again. Never in her imagination had she foreseen a proposal from a barefoot man with pens in his pocket. Her aunts and Amma had always made clear that their choice of a husband for her would be a cousin or someone related to her.

"You would make a perfect bride for me." Kandasamy's voice broke into Rasamah's reverie. "I found out your date and time of birth. I gave it, together with mine, to the priest at our temple who is also an expert astrologer."

"Oh Kadavulai, my God. What research have you been doing to get to know me? Tell me!" She tugged at the tassels over the sofa's rolled arm.

"That I cannot reveal. The scent from the fresh flowers and incense from your prayer room is still in my nose. You must have been brought up very well to make a good housewife."

"You don't understand. I have no idea what Retnam would have to say about you."

"Who is that, and what has that fellow got to do with my proposal?"

"He's my first cousin. His father is my mother's older brother. Therefore, he has a stronger claim for my hand."

Kandasamy looked so serious that it reminded her of Mother Superior, in whose presence she and her classmates were always obedient. "I don't drink or gamble and have never had a girlfriend. If you refuse me, I'll turn around and walk towards the sea and I won't stop until I drown."

Rasamah asked, "Is that from the *Ramayana*, the *Mahabharata*? I don't wish to be blamed."

"You mean you will say yes?"

"Not at all." She shook her palm.

"Say yes, and I'll take you with me to Malaya."

"Malaya?" Rasamah didn't think she could be further astonished. "What's your connection with that faraway country?"

"I have a permanent job there as a government clerk with an assured pension. If we marry, we can get much bigger government quarters reserved for married clerks." Kandasamy's chest, Rasamah noticed, seemed to swell. She got up to rush to the kitchen. She needed time to think. "Malaya?"

She returned carrying three of the kolukattai arranged on a banana leaf. "I just made them this morning."

"I will take them for my mother, who likes them, because this is an auspicious day and," he paused, "most of all, because they are from you."

Rasamah ignored the compliment. "My spiritual mother at school always spoke well of Malaya. She told us many stories about the convent on Pineapple Hill, the first place she was sent to work." Then, catching herself, she added, "I notice that you think about your mother."

"I live in Kuala Lumpur. I can take you to that hill," Kandasamy said. She could hear his words rushing out excitedly. "But now I am only on a very short, most rare and expensive home leave so if you please, I would like your correct answer as soon as possible."

Rasamah walked quickly to the front door. "I have to consult Amma, Lord Ganesha and others first."

Kandasamy bowed to say goodbye.

She watched his departing back, her mind already awhirl with thoughts. Correct answer; what a peremptory way he had about him. Such presumption!

So what is my correct answer? I shall first check what Retnam's intentions are.

The barefoot man has to wait.

When Kandasamy reached home, he carefully placed the package of kolukattai on the table. Then, he dusted the sand from his feet and wiped the perspiration from his face and arms with the cloth slung over his shoulder. He looked at the chair that had been his father's, then sat down. Kandasamy mused, "I remember Appa carving this chair from a block of tamarind wood. He and Amma worked so hard growing the rice we ate and the tobacco they sold to pay for my studies that they never had anything for themselves, not even time. I could never disappoint Amma or the spirit of Appa."

At that very moment, his mother came in carrying a banana leaf piled high with rice. As she placed it on the table she said she would fetch the curry from the cooking fire, but caught sight of Rasamah's package as she turned.

"What's this?" she asked in Tamil.

Kandasamy unwrapped the leaf to show the three cakes.

"So," said Mrs Sangarapillai, "my son has become a secret cook in Malaya and not the government worker he told me he was?"

"No, Amma, it's from the girl I spent my home leave asking about."

"So tasty." Mrs Sangarapillai bit off a piece. "She can cook well; a good omen. She is either well-brought-up or a cunning girl, bribing Amma."

Kandasamy watched his mother's face break into a broad smile. He knew that when she turned her back quickly, tears would mingle with the smile on her face. He would leave her, and she would be alone. Meanwhile, the food was cooking fragrantly on the hearth. She brought the idiyappam and sothi she had prepared and placed them carefully on the leaf before him, adding an extra scoop of the yellow spiced coconut curry for the son who wanted to be a bridegroom.

After he had eaten, Kandasamy took some dried tobacco leaves from the sack in the corner of the room to roll into a cheroot. He took a twig from the cooking fire and sat back down in his father's chair, smoking as he had watched his father do after a long day's work. His thoughts went first to his own work. Even though marriage would be a perfect reason to delay his return and he would bring back the evidence of his truthfulness in the form of his new bride, Kandasamy would never think of asking his department director for an extension of his leave. How different his life would be with a wife by his side. No more shared bachelor rooms; married officials were entitled to their own houses. A house like his bride's here in Karai Nagar, Ceylon; a home away from home which his wife would keep clean and tidy, his breakfast waiting before he left for work and his dinner ready when he returned. She would be up at 5am to perform her prayers and bless him with a vibhuti on his forehead. Kandasamy smiled at this picture of domestic bliss to come, then quickly said to himself, "But of course, I will make sure that my wife will want for nothing. She will have as many sarees as she wants: yes, a silk saree in temple blue to highlight her delicate skin, with the bluest sapphires for her ears and neck and a red pottu round as the full moon in Karai Nagar. Everything she wants. I will work hard and if I am fortunate enough to be promoted, then Amma will get a proper cooking stove and piped water."

After breakfast, Rasamah heard the vegetable seller outside their kitchen. She saw Amma standing close to the woman, listening to her gossip while she chose tapioca sticks, brinjals and chillies. Rasamah stood with one foot on the floor and the other pressed against the carved pillar of the archway between the dining room and the kitchen. She could just about hear what the vegetable seller was saying.

"All village talking vella ponnu, going to get married."

Amma didn't respond.

Rasamah went outside to see if she could hear more. As she came down the steps, she saw the vendor pull a chequered cloth over her vegetables and start off down the path towards the gate. Rasamah caught up with her to pass her the note she had written, along with a few coins. "Give this to my cousin Retnam and don't gossip about it to Amma."

A day later, Rasamah was picking hibiscus and jasmine flowers for the pooja room when she saw Kandasamy facing her across the other side of her flowering hedge. Rasamah glanced around her; Amma was back in the kitchen. Kandasamy's moustache was more pronounced under the rays from the sun. He leant over the fence and picked some jasmine. Instead of handing it to her or fastening it to her hair, he told her to add it to the garlands for the pooja room.

Kandasamy held the tray for her while she collected the last of the flowers she needed for decoration. *Why does my heart feel as if it were pounding rice grains when I look at this man?*

"Do you have the right answer for me today?" he finally asked.

Rasamah determinedly took to arranging the flowers neatly in her tray without looking at Kandasamy. "How can I decide anything when I know nothing about you? We are talking about the whole of my life in a country I don't know. You should ask your question to my mother, not to me."

There was no answer from Kandasamy for a few minutes, so she stole a quick look. He appeared to be mulling over her question. "Have you told her about my visit and my offer?"

"You think it's easy to tell my mother that a man she doesn't know wants to take me to a faraway country where she might never see me again, ignoring all tradition? I suspect someone might have told her about you."

Kandasamy seemed delighted by this. "If your mother already knows, then you can get her permission today. We can marry on an auspicious day next week and leave for Malaya at once. With the time the journey to Malaya takes, my vacation is almost finished."

Rasamah snatched the tray back from Kandasamy's hands. "Oh, you are in a hurry. You must find a wife by the end of your vacation, mustn't you?"

Kandasamy smiled and said, "You must trust me. Now I must go to make arrangements with the temple priests."

Rasamah was amazed at his audacity. Before she could tell him about her own plans to teach, he was already disappearing down the road.

Rasamah found Amma in the kitchen selecting ingredients from the spice box in preparation for the next meal. She inhaled the aroma of cinnamon, clove and pepper as Amma lifted the silver cover. Sliced onions and ginger glistened on a wooden chopping board. Amma poured oil into a pot over a lit stove. Rasamah feared it might not be the right time to tell her the news about Kandasamy's visit. But if not now, when? The urgency with which he seemed to have dispatched himself to the temple priests made her fear that word would get to Amma if she took too long, and then the decision would be wrested from her. She didn't really feel she could say yes. Imagine Mrs Dr Retnam, languishing away having tea with other doctors' wives instead of teaching.

"Amma...I have something to tell you." Rasamah stood half-hidden behind the archway at the entrance, her head peeking into the kitchen.

Rasamah's eyes widened when Amma's hands trembled. She noticed that her mother had scraped off not just the skin but also the flesh of the tapioca she was holding.

"Neighbours talking about a man visiting my house. Rasamah, you have always been too trusting." Amma spoke in Tamil the whole time, scraping even harder, making the bracelets around her wrists jangle.

"Uh...yes, Amma. Kandasamy came to ask me..."

"Kandasamy? That's his name?"

Rasamah came in to lean against the worktable where Amma was.

"What question does he dare to ask you directly?" Amma glared at her.

"Only one question. That's all he did." She looked down.

"If four people see, what will they say?"

"Amma, you are such a Tamil Tamilian. Why exactly four people, not one, two, three or five?" Rasamah scooped up some tapioca skin.

"Don't talk like a lawyer or arithmetic teacher to me," Amma said, shaking the skinless tapioca.

"Sorry, Amma."

Amma returned to chopping the ends of the rest of the tapioca.

"Actually Amma, the more people know, the better it is; Amma won't need to send our relatives from house to house informing people."

Amma rested the wrist holding the peeler on the edge of the table, her chest rapidly rising and falling. Then Amma spoke, raising her voice by notches even as the words tumbled out. "All marriages in Jaffna must be arranged. You have known this all your life. I taught you this. There is no going against tradition with such an important custom."

When Rasamah asked Amma if some rules could be bent, Amma brandished the peeler at Rasamah.

"Generations after us will be cursed and haunted by our ancestors' spirits."

"Amma, the world is changing."

"When you were small, every time Amma combed your hair, you would make it untidy again."

"I am independent, Amma."

"You have always been more gullible than independent," Amma continued.

"Amma…he says he doesn't want any dowry from you."

"Rasamah, no man has ever said that in the history of Karai Nagar or even all of Jaffna. He must be a liar."

"Amma has nothing good to say of this poor Kandasamy."

"Whatever he has to say must come from his parents."

"He says he is a government clerk with a reliable salary and a pension. He wants to take me to Malaya…"

Amma squashed up the remnants of the tapioca into a wilting piece of banana leaf.

Rasamah saw that Amma was too upset to discuss Kandasamy's proposal just then. *Best to let her calm down first.* Rasamah left the kitchen on the pretext of going to weave a flower garland.

As Rasamah was on the way to her bedroom, a maid pressed a piece of folded paper she said was from Mr Retnam's gardener into her palm.

Unfolding it quickly, she read,

I need to study medicine in Colombo. I can't take anyone with me while on serious business. No distractions while I fulfil my parents' ambitions for me. Many mothers in Colombo regularly visit the medical faculty of the university to select suitable husbands for their daughters. I will get many invitations, some difficult to refuse if the parents are very important. Your proposer, Kandasamy I heard, is most determined. With your dream of travel to Malaya and my chance to be a doctor, I am forced to step aside for Kandasamy. I hope you understand.

Your cousin

Dr-to-be Retnam

Rasamah read the letter again. She shredded the note into pieces and threw it into the wastepaper basket. She took the Colombo doll that Retnam had given her when they were kids from her pillow and hurled it through her bedroom window; it landed on some horse dung.

"So," Rasamah swore, "that's all I mean to you?"

Rasamah was engrossed in clearing her parents' travel trunk. She tiptoed to reach the cupboard's top shelf to choose the cotton sarees. She selected both those in bright and pastel shades before deciding on matching slippers and sandals from the lower shelf of her cupboard. She inhaled the aroma of Amma's sandalwood; Amma was at her door.

"Why are you rushing to pack?" Amma asked.

"Even the humble vegetable seller and boys younger than me were allowed to cross the bridge to the next island, but Amma forbade me." Rasamah stretched the straps inside the smaller leather suitcase to knot them.

"Where do you want to run to?" Amma walked into her room and faced her.

She pretended not to notice that Amma was still angry, a trick she had used on the nuns at the convent. "Amma, I am considering going to Malaya with Kandasamy."

"Your aunty in Colombo is talking about marriage with a doctor boy there. With a doctor son-in-law, my boastful cousin with an engineer son-in-law will keep quiet." Amma held Rasamah's hand.

"A doctor?" Rasamah stamped her foot. "Amma, are you saying this just to stop me from marrying Kandasamy?"

"Doctor boy's proposal, take plenty of time, money also." Amma opened the trunk to remove her school certificates on the top layer, but Rasamah snatched them back.

"Shall I stay in this village–prison when I have a handsome rescuer?" Rasamah chose coloured bangles from the dressing-table drawer.

"Aiyo, Rasamah, I am talking about Colombo doctor, you want low, low, clerk from Malaya?" Amma staggered towards the teak chair next to her.

Rasamah dropped the bangles, which rolled in different directions on the floor, to grab Amma's elbow. "But I could be a teacher like Mother Superior."

"Rasamah, you know our custom. If not Retnam, then an arranged doctor. You don't understand status, property, money, caste…" Amma looked her in the eye. "Cousins marrying cousins are all arranged at the time of birth. I want to give a grand wedding for you."

Rasamah sat Amma down on her bed. "Amma, rotten Retnam wants me to wait for six long years for him without any promises."

Seeing Amma wipe her eyes, Rasamah dabbed Amma's cheeks with her shawl.

"There are ready-made doctors in Colombo."

"But none of them has proposed to take me away from here, unlike Kandasamy."

"Within hours of the midwife leaving after I delivered you, I had the astrologer and the priest cast your horoscope. There is no way I will allow this Kandasamy to change these rules or set foot in my home again." Amma removed Rasamah's fingers, which she had plugged into her ears.

"In Malaya, maybe I could be like Mother Superior and teach in the school on Pineapple Hill that he promised to show me."

"Young men from Malaya, returning on home leave to marry, promised their new brides a fancy life. When they went to Malaya, their wives were called 'village women'," Amma said.

"Once I am a school teacher, who will dare call me a village woman, Amma?"

"Your uncles said these wives were left at home while their husbands drank, gambled and came home late in the night."

"Amma, you know the men here are worse. Kandasamy himself neither drinks nor gambles, and most of all he doesn't want Amma's property."

"That Kandasamy's family is so poor. Forget him, Rasamah." Amma shook her head.

"Is money so important, Amma?"

"Your future life must be as good as or better than it is now."

Amma pointed to the sarees from Kanchipuram to Banares, the matching embroidered blouses, the beaded slippers and the pairs of bejewelled pavadai thavani in myriad colours with matching shawls before she flung open the left side of the cupboard where the jewellery boxes were stacked.

"Doctors will be prosperous."

"As any doctor's wife, I would be in silk sarees and gold bracelets gossiping with other doctors' idle wives. I'd rather be a busy schoolteacher."

"You would be a wife trapped inside a clerk husband's house."

"I am a girl caged in Amma's house. It can't be worse?"

"This man will never be a doctor, and government servants are still servants."

"But he will be proud to have a teacher wife. With both of us working we can afford to travel."

"Retnam will travel to England."

"Amma, six long years later, if he graduates as a doctor. This man has travelled to and from Malaya."

She took out the framed picture of Mother Superior signed with the words, "Rasamah, you will make a great teacher." She shared with Amma that she hoped to see the wild tigers that Mother Superior enthused about.

"I hope you won't be faced with a wild husband instead."

Amma seized the photo of Mother Superior from Rasamah and threw it on the floor. Rasamah picked it up and brushed it down with her fingers before placing it within the pile of sarees. "I don't think Kandasamy will do such a thing."

"What do you know about him?"

"He's better looking than Retnam."

"Like a silly girl you think that's all that matters."

"I won't be a silly daughter chained to my mother's house

until some drinking and beating man comes to claim my Amma's property with me as an excuse."

Rasamah held up her book prizes for English literature.

"Are you going to use your *English* on your kitchen pots and pans?"

"Amma, you didn't let me improve your broken English. I can make up for it by teaching many pupils in Malaya."

"It's all right, I am most proud to speak only in Tamil."

In response, Rasamah lifted the shawl of Amma's saree and began to twirl it, something she did to seek her mother's permission before going out. As Amma left her room, Rasamah heard her mother grumbling that even the Mother Superior couldn't control a wild girl like her.

Later that day, Rasamah saw Kandasamy approaching as she helped Amma tend to the flowers on their patio.

"Vanakam, Mrs Chinnathamby." Kandasamy bowed.

"Deh, how dare you propose directly to my daughter? Have you no shame?" Amma shouted as she walked down the stairs to the front porch.

"So very sorry about the way I did it, because I had to rush to get a customary bride from our home country." He lifted his pressed palms.

"Thousand years' tradition, you dare to change?"

For the first time, Rasamah saw Amma rise tall despite her small build. Amma did not even invite him to sit down, let alone offer him a cup of Ceylon tea. Kandasamy was left standing on the porch. Amma caught Rasamah's wrist and was about to pull her into the house when she saw Kandasamy kneel. Rasamah recoiled from seeing Amma slam the door shut on Kandasamy.

As Kandasamy walked back home, he looked towards the sea. He felt he could not be absent from his office any longer than the duration of his approved leave. He needed to relate the encounter to his mother to gauge how she could help him quickly overcome the rejection from Mrs Chinnathamby.

His mother held his arm. "How upset she must have been to have some buffalo fresh from Malaya blunder into her house and threaten to take away her only daughter. Let me take you back to her house. You say nothing. I will speak in our proper way, mother to mother," Mrs Sangarapillai said.

Kandasamy cleaned their bullock cart for the journey and spread a blanket on the cart's floorboard.

Early next morning when Mrs Chinnathamby saw Mrs Sangarapillai, she invited her in, seated her on the sofa and told the maids to bring tea and payasam. Kandasamy trailed behind his mother.

"This one doesn't know the proper way to make a marriage proposal. He's not respecting the elders." Mrs Chinnathamby glared at Kandasamy before pointing to the portraits of Rasamah's father, grandparents and great-grandparents hanging in her sitting room. "All of them maintained the traditions lasting thousands of years. I will never allow Rasamah to even dream of casting away our customs," she continued.

"I'm correcting him now," Mrs Sangarapillai said.

"He can crouch behind other suitors."

Mrs Sangarapillai told Mrs Chinnathamby that her son didn't want her money or her plantations. Mrs Chinnathamby raised her eyebrows, saying she might believe this only if Kandasamy wrote that down and signed, the way Rasamah's father would have wanted.

In the adjoining room, Rasamah's eyes grew round at how businesslike her mother was being. With the issue of dowry settled, Mrs Chinnathamby turned to horoscopes and the couple's suitability for each other. Kandasamy's mother assured Mrs Chinnathamby that priests from Amman, Murugan and Pillayar had said that all matched fully.

When she heard Kandasamy's mother saying, "All the Gods are on his side", Rasamah licked her finger and made a large tick in the air.

"Another correct answer," Rasamah whispered to herself.

After Kandasamy and his mother had left, their tea and payasam untouched, Mrs Chinnathamby promptly sent her carriage to the three temples mentioned by Kandasamy's mother and invited the priests to visit her "on urgent business". Each priest in turn confirmed that the horoscopes showed the couple was indeed compatible. Even the difficulty of Amma being a widow and unable to perform a full marriage ceremony was no barrier; the Chief Priest from the Pillayar temple advised Amma that if she sat on a muram filled with rice padi during the marriage ceremony, it would be permissible for her to give Rasamah away. After the priests had left, Rasamah turned to her mother and said, "Amma, this change in my life seems fated."

"Which man," her mother looked into Rasamah's face, "can put up with my stubborn daughter?" Amma's eyes filled with tears.

Rasamah felt they were tears of anger mixed with sadness.

That very evening Rasamah's aunts and her cousins gathered at Rasamah's house. Amma's youngest sister sketched intricate floral patterns with henna paste on Rasamah's forearms, palms, toes and shins. Amma asked if she would get half as much pampering from Kandasamy in Malaya.

The next day Rasamah stepped out of her bedroom dressed in a red-and-gold silk saree. The strings of jasmine strung through Rasamah's plaited hair filled the room with their fragrance. In the middle of Rasamah's forehead hung a glistening red ruby, a gift from Amma.

"Although you go with no dowry, you shall have ample jewellery." Mrs Chinnathamby slipped three heavy gold bangles onto each of Rasamash's wrists. She slowly opened a red velvet box; inside, a pair of pearl and diamond earrings glistened as they caught the sunlight. "These," she said, "my mother gave me on my wedding day and now my only daughter will take them with her on her new life, in her new country, with her new husband."

"Amma, thank you." Tears filled Rasamah's eyes as she clasped Amma's wrists. As Amma reached up to place the earrings in Rasamah's ears, Rasamah heard a cluster of aunts and cousins discussing the success of the ponnuruku ceremony in Kandasamy's home, where the goldsmith melted the gold for the thali. The party moved outside the house to where coconuts were ritually thrown against a stone. As each fruit smashed, scattering water and pieces of shattered coconut around the courtyard, Amma smiled at her daughter, "Every nut smashed, and so just like this broken fruit, nothing will now stand in your path to happiness, no obstacle in your future life."

The wedding ceremony progressed. Amma took Rasamah's right hand and offered it to Kandasamy. Rasamah felt the firmness of Kandasamy's hand. She sat with him on the manavarai decorated with fresh flowers, colourful twinkling lights and velvet cushions. The priest began the ritual of throwing twigs from the mango tree and saucers of ghee into the fire. As Rasamah watched the flames flicker, she began to have doubts. *Which heat will my life be? Will it be the heat of passion and happiness or something else? What will two people make of their lives together? What will my future life hold?*

Kandasamy reached across and tied the thali string around Rasamah's neck. Rasamah remembered their very first meeting, when the neighing of her pony had brought her out from the kitchen. It seemed like yesterday, and now here she was getting married. The beat rose from the mridangam and the flute tune soared. Rasamah reached back for Amma's fingers. Saffron rice grains, jasmine petals and rosewater covered Amma's touch.

Rasamah and Kandasamy shared a tumbler of warm milk. Kandasamy led her around the sacred fire three times before she sat with him to have their first meal together from a single silver plate. Their male relatives sat to dine first, followed by the women. Rasamah watched the meal progress, the women getting what the men left.

"Don't spoil our Chinnathamby name with your new family." Amma hugged Rasamah and kissed her on the cheek.

"Don't worry, Amma."

"Send a telegram when you arrive in Malaya. Write letters about how he takes care of you." Rasamah's eyes swelled as Amma dabbed her own.

Rasamah saw Amma standing apart from their relatives and friends, as if she wanted to be alone to say a silent goodbye to her daughter. In her widow-white saree, Amma would now be alone in the family bungalow. "My dear Amma, when will I see you again?" Rasamah turned to look at Kandasamy, who was gazing eagerly at the shore and the relatives waving on the dock.

This man is my future now and I must follow where he takes me.

The waves carried the reflection of the last of the setting sun; lights began to twinkle from the shore. Furrows widened behind the ship as it steamed on its way to Malaya. Rasamah's grip on the deck rail tightened as the full realisation of what she had done gushed over her like a wave. Now that the excitement of the proposal and marriage was over, here she was, sailing away from everything she knew, having put her whole life and well-being into the hands of a stranger. She slipped her fingers beneath Kandasamy's elbow, and he turned to look at her. She saw that although his eyes were serious in thought, his face smiled gently at her.

The ship began to move away from the dock, but even the loudness of its horn could not drown out Rasamah's thought that there was now no turning back.

MARRIAGE AND MUTTON CURRY

COURT HILL, KUALA LUMPUR

Bloody fountain pens, Rasamah muttered.

She scoured the smears on the pocket of Kandasamy's white office shirt.

How those pens confused me when Athan first came to Amma's house and I looked at his bare feet. What kind of man could this be? I should have known that those pens were a red warning sign when he started writing for his work during our second night on the ship to Penang.

Rasamah raised her head to glance out through the metal lattice protecting the window.

Shall I talk to those green coconut palms I see more often than I do Athan? His big romance is work and until I can start teaching, this is mine. It's time to get to know my neighbours. Who will be first? Mrs Chong on my right or Mrs Chelvi Chellapah on my left? Mrs Chong is tending to a baby, so she might like some help but might be too busy to chat, otherwise she would have come in to see us when we moved in. I see Mrs Chellapah sitting on her doorstep at all hours of the day until her husband comes home.

Rasamah rinsed the pure white shirt, now free of stains, under the cold-water tap above the cement sink where she placed the tubful of washing.

But how well will I get along with a woman who ties her saree so that everyone can see her ankles? Why, those women in the temple last Friday said this Mrs Chellapah hadn't even finished secondary school and she is a Jaffna Tamil—what a disgrace. But we can start by going to the market and cooking together. Everyone likes thosai and mutton curry. I could start my teaching with her. I cannot leave my ambition to teach, not just because it is something I would enjoy but because the extra money is the way to get what I enjoy most—seeing places, meeting people.

That evening, Kandasamy carried his work files into the study. Rasamah tiptoed behind him. In her bedroom, she took a brown manila envelope from her leather suitcase and slid out her school certificates. With a smile, she read the letter of recommendation Mother Superior had given her on her final day at school, her voice telling Rasamah that teaching was the highest profession. Looking down into the suitcase, she lifted a bundle of books tied together and undid the bow on the white string. She chose one exercise book—English literature—and turned the pages over, looking at her favourite poems and the scribbled marks of "Excellent" in the teacher's green ink at the bottom of each page. She remembered fondly the nun who had given her a well-thumbed *Guide to Training* of the Church of Ireland College of Education with the remark, "Such a clever girl should pass on her cleverness to others." At the bottom of the pile was a group of pencil drawings she had made in the art class—pictures from magazines of churches set along cobbled streets in Dublin, Belfast and Rome. Rasamah rolled them together and put the tube to her eye.

Do I see a Malayan tiger? Maybe Penang? And is that Dublin, with its grand Cathedral of Our Lady in the distance?

She flattened out the drawings and re-tied the books and papers into a bundle to place back into the suitcase. She looked through her school certificates one by one.

How shall I express my desire to teach?
She pulled a sheet of white paper towards her.

When Kandasamy returned from work the next day she served him tea and murukku, which she started frying the minute the key turned in the door. She listened as he bit into the crisp delicacy and adjourned to his study, his papers rolled under his arm. Those papers might as well have been love letters, the way he guarded and read them in secret.

What happened to the man who would have walked into the sea if I had refused to marry him? What happened to the unexpected touch on my neck as I stood cooking? Or the way his hands covered my eyes when he first showed me around the house. Although this house, one in a row of houses just like it, was nothing like Amma's, it had been filled with laughter when we arrived. Now it is steeped in silence with bundles of paper tied with red tape. The clothes I wore that day, the lilac saree and gold shawl, are folded away in the cupboard. When I joked that the menfolk would never know which house to go into if they came home after drinking too much, Kandasamy only said that if they had the sense to stop at their first glass of liquor, they wouldn't make fools of themselves. So much easier to just laugh like Amma, or like Mother Superior, but then again maybe I'm lucky to have a serious husband who does know which house to come home to each night, even if it is always late when he does.

It had only been a year after they moved in to their government-issued quarters when Rasamah noticed that the paint from the outer walls was peeling off. She felt this was a great opportunity to repaint them in colours different from those of their neighbours so that it stood out from the row. Kandasamy, however, said that it was against government rules to paint the house anything other than the regulation cream walls with brown windows and doors.

But making mine stand out from the others is exactly what I want.

Rasamah placed her application to teach at the school on Pineapple Hill in the top drawer of Kandasamy's desk. He would see it as soon as he filled his fountain pens with Parker's red and blue–black Quink ink, as he did every night.

She pictured Kandasamy smiling at his wife's ambition.

Day after day, during the passing weeks, as soon as Rasamah heard the serious slap of Kandasamy's stout leather shoes on the bottom veranda step, she began cooking the meal she had spent the day preparing. Each morning as the serious leather shoes descended the steps, Rasamah rushed into the study, hoping that today she would find that he had taken her letter off to be posted. But her letter was still there. Rasamah kept her hopes alive for many weeks, trying to nudge Kandasamy's thoughts with a myriad of small gestures. She served his favourite meals. She made sure his shoes gleamed when they caught the sun. She made kolukattai, hoping that Kandasamy would recall how she had given him this sweet on their first meeting. Kandasamy ate the treats and laced the shoes up. The letter remained in his top drawer.

One evening, she decided to make a direct approach. He settled into an armchair with the newspaper spread out in front of him. Rasamah crossed the room to his desk and took out her letter. Ankle bells tinkling, she walked over to place the letter on top of the page he was reading.

"I want to apply for my teaching job soon, Athan."

"Don't trouble." He didn't look up from his reading.

"Why not, Athan?"

Kandasamy threw the newspaper onto a side table.

Rasamah watched her certificates and testimonials fly across the floor with the discarded sheets of newsprint. She stooped to gather them up before sorting the newspapers back.

"Am I so desperate that I need my wife to earn?"

Rasamah hugged her application letter to her chest. "Athan, if you had read my notes in your drawer you wouldn't have cast them or me into one corner."

He rolled the newspaper and whacked it over the arm on his chair. She jerked back.

Rasamah saw the glint of Kandasamy's glasses as they fell from the table. She picked them up, wiped them with the tip of her saree shawl and replaced them into their hard case. She couldn't forget the telling-off she'd received when he found the case empty once—only to find the glasses in his study later. This was one of her duties: to replace his glasses in their case for him.

"I should have made you promise me that I could be a school-teacher in Malaya before I agreed to marry you. When Amma said I am so naïve and trusting, I didn't listen." Seeing Kandasamy's moustache bristle, she added, "Athan needn't have to work long hours, and we could have more time…together." Rasamah put one hand to her cheek and found it burning hot.

"If you go out to earn, our community will think I cannot support my own wife. It is below my dignity to let them think that of me. I cannot allow you to work for money."

"Teaching is not working for money. It is a vocation like being a doctor. Where is the shame in that? Surely the community understands that. They respect teachers. Where is the harm? And my desires mean nothing, Athan?"

Rasmah saw Kandasamy's brows furrow and his frown deepen.

"Athan, I don't want to be like Chelvi and the other housewives."

"You are far above them…you know that."

She wanted to say that it was even more reason for her to work but didn't dare to.

"Without my self-respect as a senior government clerk, I am nothing. You can improve our house and garden, teach your friend here."

Kandasamy got up and went to the bedroom. The slam of the door echoed in the house. Rasamah placed her application between the sarees in her clothes cupboard. Would she dare send it herself and if she did, could she risk the damage to her marriage?

He mentioned teaching her neighbour Mrs Chelvi Chellapah. Rasamah disdained Chelvi's lack of education; Rasamah's education certainly made her stand out among the other wives. Could she really take on the education of Mrs Chellapah? Would this be the stepping stone to something bigger and better? Rasamah pondered the thought as she heated up the gingelly oil with fenugreek seeds for Athan's massage. *At least there is no whiff of whiskey on him, unlike on Chelvi's husband.*

"Chelvi, look," Rasamah bent over to inhale the fragrance from a neem plant shooting up near the wall around her house. "Amma told me to grow it closest to the house. The breeze blowing through its branches prevents sickness."

"Acca, your family how many girls and boys?" asked Chelvi.

"I am the only girl." She paused before adding, "But my aunt has four daughters; when she called, 'girl and girl go there and girl and girl stay here', they knew exactly who should do what."

"How, Acca…?" She saw Chelvi's mouth remaining agape.

"My aunt disciplined them so well that they knew, just by looking into her eyes, what her instructions were."

"How about you, Acca?"

"Me, no problem, I was away at the convent and escaped Amma's training, and was rarely allowed to go anywhere. Chelvi, which part of Jaffna are you from?"

"From Kayts."

"Kadavulai, that's just next door to my Karai Nagar. We are neighbours here again. Shall we be friends as well?"

Lord Ganesha, thank you! Rasamah touched the sides of her face before raising her clasped palms above her forehead. *It is miraculous to arrive in a strange country and to find that the first person I meet is someone from my neighbouring village in Jaffna, no less.*

"I need one friend also." Chelvi grinned.

Craning back so that she almost touched the garden's paling regulation-white perimeter fence, Rasamah gazed at the profusion of yellow allamanda and purple bougainvillea that brought a distinctive touch of colour to the cream walls of her regulation government quarters. Among the branches, yellow-vented bulbuls pecked and sucked at the blossoms, whistling a welcome to the garden. Rasamah dipped her fingers into the tea dust pressed into the coconut shell she carried and sprinkled the dust onto the leaves of the tulasi plant in its copper urn, taking pride of place on her veranda.

I may not have the chandeliers and embroidered cushions from Robinsons and other expensive shops, but even the doctor cousin whom Kandasamy took me to meet when we first arrived doesn't have such beautiful colours around his house, nor the fragrance of this jasmine around the window frames nor the spirituality of my beautiful tulasi plant, which cares for us all.

Touching the leaves of the tulasi as she went back into the house, she plucked a leaf to place gently between her lips. It dropped from her mouth as she entered the kitchen and saw Chelvi squatting on the red-tiled floor next to the cooking stove.

"Sit here, Chelvi." Rasamah pointed to a bright-blue chair, one of the four she had painted and placed around the kitchen table. "I don't want to splash you with this boiling milk. Have you tasted Ceylon tea made with fresh milk recently?"

"I drink without milk, Acca."

She wondered if she would ever change Chelvi's village habits and her expectation to be beneath everyone else. Rasamah poured sugared nuts from a glass jar into a plain white saucer and placed them in front of Chelvi.

"Try these too. My mother always likes some sweets with her tea."

How could Chelvi not thank her hostess?

"I come your house to ask you to show me how you cook mutton curry and nasi biryani. Mr Chellapah always complain, complain about my food. You have the ingredients, yes? You can show me in English then I can learn more also."

Rasamah looked at the sugar from the nuts adhering to Chelvi's top lip and silently changed her planned dinner menu to mutton curry with nasi biryani.

"Listen to the song you teach me," Chelvi chimed in, "May… ree had a little lamp, little lamp, little lamp, May…ree had a little lamp, its fleece was white as snow."

"Lovely singing voice," Rasamah said. "Although I'm not sure how much curry we can make with lamps."

Chelvi stretched out her hand to take the few remaining nuts from the saucer. Rasamah's eyes opened wide as she looked down at the row of green-and-brown bruises that ran the whole length of Chelvi's arm. "How did you get these?" Rasamah asked, pointing to the bumps.

Chelvi dropped her chin onto her chest and muttered, "Last night. Mr Chellapah eating all the food, rice, egg, chicken, drinking beer from bottle. I went to take little rice, like this, only."

She held up her thumb and finger for Rasamah's inspection, "and Mr Chellapah pull me from table and throw me on the floor. I got no dinner only free bottles for flowers."

Rasamah remembered her mother's doubts when she had first found out about Kandasamy, and the stories she told of the girls from Karai Nagar and the surrounding villages who were taken off to Malaya as proud wives, only to find that they had wedded themselves to a life as a servant, cleaning and cooking, with the added burden of bearing children.

So, what Amma said is true for some. Even if I only have a garden to take care of, I must be very grateful that my Kandasamy is not like this.

Rasamah turned to Chelvi. "I won't let that devil smack you about, Chelvi," she said. This promise elicited a hug from Chelvi.

"Thank you, Acca, you my guard and angel and surely you not carry tales to gossipers at our temple."

"And if you want mutton curry we had better go quickly to the market before the lamp, I mean lamb, is all sold." On a whim, Rasamah stroked her friend's shoulder. "Let's take a rickshaw to the market." She jiggled the beaded purse. "I want to post a letter to my Amma."

Chelvi looked frightened. "If I am late returning home, I will get a beating."

"But what about the mutton curry and biryani?" Rasamah gave her a bigger hug and led her outside.

Rasamah held up her hand to hail a rickshaw puller.

When they arrived at the post office, Rasamah took two envelopes from her bag: one addressed to Amma, the other to the principal of the Convent Bukit Nanas. She stood outside holding both letters for a long time before putting the Convent Bukit Nanas letter back in her bag with a heavy sigh. When she returned to the rickshaw, she found Chelvi's eyes were wet.

Rasamah asked the now crying Chelvi why she was in such a hurry to prepare lunch on a workday when their husbands would take lunch at the office.

"No office today. Drink so much beer. This morning I dare not wake him. He is there." Chelvi pointed as if Chellapah were seated next to her.

Rasamah turned towards the rickshaw man and promised to double her agreed fare if he could run all the way back to the government quarter. The man panted as he pulled the two women up the rise leading into the housing area. To distract Chelvi, Rasamah explained how one day she had asked a rickshaw puller in her broken bazaar Malay if he could teach her a few words of Malay and Cantonese in return for some English. From him, she learned how to say "what news?" in Malay and "have you eaten rice?" in Cantonese, along with some other words.

"Aiyo, they use bad words in Malay and bad, bad words in Cantonese for greeting each other," Chelvi explained.

"Why you didn't tell me this earlier?" Rasamah tugged Chelvi's sleeve. Chelvi told her what some of the other words meant, making Rasamah laugh so much that the rickshaw jolted even more. "You are a darling for making me laugh, my dear Chelvi. What will I do without you?"

The rickshaw slowed down in front of her house, and there was no more talk. Rasamah paid the sweating rickshaw man. As she watched Chelvi jump down to scuttle off to her house, almost dropping her basket of shopping on the way, Rasamah looked at the neem plant. *Will you keep me healthy? What if I were ill, what would Kandasamy do? Would he leave his work and stay home to look after me?* Rasamah shivered slightly as she climbed the stairs back into the house.

The aroma of the spices drew Kandasamy from his study.

Rasamah moved across to the dining table and turned over the china plates she had left inverted on the white tablecloth so that flies wouldn't walk on them. She brought from the kitchen a steaming pot of rice, a bowl filled with the sweet-and-sour pacheri and finally, a brimming bowl of fragrant curry. She put down three scoopfuls of rice and covered it with a ladleful of rich curry. She watched Kandasamy mash the curry into the rice with potatoes chopped into small cubes and fried with garlic and onion, and she remembered Chelvi's words. "Good thing I am not your daughter-in-law, made to slice every vegetable perfect, perfect."

He took a bite of the edge of a fried papadum, which she brought out from a used Jacob & Co. cream-cracker tin. Apart from the crackling, he ate silently. In the early days of their marriage, Kandasamy liked to say, "Hotel chefs would be put to shame!"

"Athan, we don't need to have meals without speaking as the nuns at my school did."

Kandasamy looked up from his food. Rasamah could not make out if a smile was hidden beneath his moustache. She reminisced about dinnertime with Amma back home. As she talked, the aromas of her mother's kitchen came back and she heard the sound of the waves beating on the shore near her childhood home.

Rasamah was about to replace the annual wall calendar from Ganesha Silk Sarees with a new one for the fifth time when Kandasamy said that they had been allotted government quarters for higher-rank staff at Scott Road, Brickfields. She hugged Kandasamy on hearing that Chelvi would continue to be her neighbour. She rushed out towards Chelvi's house and called out to her. When Chelvi came out, she hugged her, kissed her on both cheeks, before swaying her left and right in a dance. "Hooray, you are going to be my neighbour again in our new, bigger quarter. I will cook mutton curry, biryani, rasa velli kilangu and much more for you as part of our big celebration."

The money she received from Kandasamy to buy a pair of gold earrings or a necklace, she spent on choosing cushion covers, embroidered chair backs and multi-coloured bathroom rugs. She was proud of her furnishings, of how the woven braid gleamed in the morning's sun through her lace curtains, a touch of so-phistication so lacking in the other houses along the row. A lamp stand carved with elephants added a touch of homeliness next to Kandasamy's favourite chair. Her new garden, although smaller than Amma's, flourished with jasmine flowers, ferns, jackfruit and banana plants.

One morning, while sitting in the garden, Chelvi said, "Acca, temple ladies giving me nice title, 'simpleton'."

"I hope you didn't thank them. It wasn't a compliment." Rasamah waved the shrivelled ferns she had just snipped off.

"I grateful to you, Acca. You teach me new things always."

Rasamah picked a single hibiscus to place it between the hairpins on Chelvi's kondai.

"Look, Acca, worms attacking, one, two…six buds, all *blaack aready*," said Chelvi.

"They need attention just like us." Rasamah pulled out the musty leaves with mould and pests while pruning the hibiscus bushes.

"Don't be such a flower pot, Acca."

"You mean fussy pot?"

Chelvi giggled.

"Acca, no need to be sad, our *quart-rers*-friends telling, 'Mrs Kandasamy is ladies' leader of our community.'"

"I started this rumour." Rasamah tilted her face upwards. The heat of the late-morning sun no longer made her pull the saree shawl over her bare neckline.

When they moved here, Kandasamy was the only "office husband" who did not know what the interior of the clubhouse looked like. "Bars and billiards for them, not me," Kandasamy said when she tried to persuade him to watch Jaffna Tamil government clerks playing cricket with their British bosses at the clubhouse.

They were to attend the Muthurajahs' anniversary dinner at the club on Saturday and she raised her pressed palms to Lord Ganesha in her pooja room, to pray Kandasamy would remember not to work a full day. Kandasamy might rush from the office direct to the club just in time, with guests gawking at him still dressed austerely in his office attire in contrast to her, dressed in jewels and sandals that fully matched the colour of her saree for this special occasion.

My travel fund is growing nicely. How far will it take me?

"Sorry lah, so late." Chelvi bustled through the door without knocking.

Rasamah quickly stuffed the bills she had been counting back into the Quality Street tin she used for housekeeping money. "Don't be known as the late Mrs Chellapah. If you have a cold, you will have a walking not a running nose."

Rasamah picked up the sponge she had left on the draining board. She shook onto it some of the ash from the burnt incense sticks she kept in a glass jar on the window ledge to begin scrubbing the aluminium pots that filled the sink. Rasamah turned when Chelvi started to cry. In between sobs, Chelvi told the story of how Chellapah threw iddli on her and how he had yelled at her, "Go, go find how Rasamah help Kandasamy to be number one in office."

Rasamah felt a wave of pity for Chelvi. Patting her friend on the cheek, she said that if Chelvi still had problems with her husband, she could come to Rasamah's house. Rasamah would leave the porch light on all night.

"But Acca, after make your electric bill jump up."

"My Athan will pay." Rasamah smiled at the thought. He had, after all, agreed enthusiastically with Rasamah's idea that she should teach Chelvi.

"Your husband good bund." Chelvi angled her chin towards Rasamah.

"You mean good man. He would be so much better if he lets me do what I want."

Rasamah offered to read to her from the *Bhagavad Gita*. Rasamah pulled out a low stool in front of her bookcase.

Chelvi hugged her, saying that Lord Ganesha had sent Rasamah to be her "best friend, kitchen, house and garden teacher".

As she read, Rasamah saw Chelvi yawn. She led Chelvi to her wardrobe and chose one light-blue saree speckled with flowers on its border. When Rasamah gave it to Chelvi, her friend shook her palms in protest. Rasamah told her that Mr Kandasamy had bought her so many sarees he wouldn't know if she gave Chelvi one.

Kandasamy returned one evening and sat down in his favourite chair. Turning on the lamp with the carved elephants, he crossed his legs. He had important news. He tapped the cushion of the easy chair facing his own when Rasamah walked in.

Rasamah pressed the crimson pottu on her forehead and rolled her damp hair up into a loose bun. "If you have good news, Athan deserves a reward."

"I am not a child that needs rewards." Kandasamy's voice was stern.

Tonight they would have special spicy mutton curry with marrow bones so rich he would eat like a king. The pineapple pacheri made with red and green chillies, just as he liked it, chillies chopped and tossed in that sweet-and-savoury salad.

"You booked tickets for our Karai Nagar or Irish trip?" She felt her spirits rise.

"Something better than that."

"Athan, what could be better?"

"My boss said my name was first on his list for promotion over more senior staff. He proposed to the State Secretariat headquarters in Jalan Raja to appoint me Division Head. I must keep it secret until the approval letter comes. You can choose something special for Deepavali."

"Athan, I have jewellery and embroidered slippers to match my sarees." She paused. "To celebrate, let's go overseas."

"Once promoted, I must work more hours. I can't apply for leave but I can give you more money to buy anything you want. I have to keep my promise to your Amma to build you a bigger house once I retire."

Back and forth they went, throughout dinner, with Rasamah arguing that they would be old if they kept putting trips off and talking about retirement. When they first arrived in Malaya, they had gone to visit Kandasamy's doctor cousin and she had seen an album of photographs of places in Europe. Places the doctor cousin had visited with his wife and seen with his own eyes. Just one trip would fill her with memories for a lifetime. Penang or Singapore would be enough to start with.

How strange it all looked when I first arrived at the dock in Penang. Georgetown looked hyperactive in contrast to our small rural Karai Island in Jaffna. I was mesmerised by the cacophony of sounds from people speaking at a fast pace and high volume. I stared from one person to the other. Kandasamy noticed this and told me how those people switched from Hokkien to Malay, from English to Tamil and some Siamese. A team of bulls hitched to bullock carts passed through, but what excited me more than that was seeing a pony cart like Amma's with an English couple riding in it. Why could Kandasamy and I not go to see my and his Amma or to Ireland, the home of Mother Superior?

"Too many 'whys', Rasamah. Think carefully. More senior staff will question why I got chosen instead of them."

"Remember, Athan, you threw custom into the sea to propose directly to me?"

"Rasamah, a man can be proud when his wife wears imported silk sarees and more than one gold chain. Better if he can afford to employ maids for house chores. All paid for with his own salary. I don't want relatives to look down on me for making you work to fill our rice bowl."

"Athan, you have always given me material comforts. What I want to do is teach, travel and talk." Rasamah turned the gold bracelets on her wrist.

Slowly, Kandasamy pushed his half-eaten plate of food away. "If I get this promotion, I will take you out. We will go for a different dinner, maybe Chinese or Malay or even European. Then a special visit to the Ganesha Saree Centre." He rose from the table and walked into the bedroom, slamming the door behind him.

Rasamah picked up the still steaming bowl of curry. In the kitchen, without a pause for thought, she scraped the curry into the waste bin.

In the months ahead, Rasamah continued to make fragrant mutton curry as monsoon rains swept through Kuala Lumpur. At first,

Rasamah faced these with all the vitality of youth, but as her disappointment grew, her resistance against the wind and rain decreased and she found it more difficult to get out of bed. Her head ached and her chest filled. The Malays had a saying—masuk angin, or "enter wind"—and she felt as if wind had filled all her cavities as she tried to fulfil each task her husband needed or wanted.

Rasamah was most grateful when Chelvi spent almost all her spare time sitting beside her by her sickbed. Chelvi first helped to twist open the metal cover of a bottle of Vicks that Kandasamy had bought and left with the seal still on. Chelvi dabbed some drops on the handkerchief for Rasamah to inhale. Rasamah breathed better and patted Chelvi's shoulder to thank her. In a moment of euphoria, Rasamah unwittingly revealed the news of her husband's promotion.

And then one day, Rasamah couldn't get out of bed.

Kandasamy, like a good civil servant, was a master of compromise. An hour later he stood by Rasamah's bedside to announce, "There is no need to worry. Tomorrow an amah will start here. She will work so you can rest to regain your strength."

Rasamah took Kandasamy's hand and placed his palm on her forehead. "Athan," she said, "so practical, but I don't want a black-and-white government maid to match your black-and-white government paper. Why can't you stay with me? Just for today?"

Kandasamy pulled his hand away. "They are called black and white because of their black trousers and white blouse. It has nothing to do with government service."

As the bedroom door closed behind Kandasamy, Rasamah inhaled deeply from the Vicks balm on her handkerchief. She started to cough and her eyes filled with water. My Chelvi, always there for me. Rasamah smiled before sleeping through the rest of the day and didn't even hear when Kandasamy returned. She managed to get up the next morning and found Kandasamy sitting at the kitchen table. An elderly Chinese woman dressed in black trousers and a white blouse with a high collar fastened up to her chin was placing a glass of tea in front of Kandasamy.

Rasamah sat down opposite Kandasamy. She wanted to say how much she missed him, but Kandasamy rose and said that he must be off to work. His heavy leather shoes clattered on the bare wooden steps outside. Rasamah spent the morning showing the maid where to find everything and went back to rest. At midday, she woke with a start to a soft knock on her bedroom door.

The maid entered. "Lunch is ready, madam. Chicken soup. Fight your fever, make you strong again."

For a week, Rasamah drank the healthy soup and got plenty of rest. Or rather she spent a long time on her own in her room, but for much of the time she didn't sleep. During her pooja sessions, her prayers became more elaborate as she put forth to Lord Ganesha all the stirrings and wishes of her heart. Lord Ganesha must have heard her prayers, for when Kandasamy came home at the end of the week and saw Rasamah in her usual place in the kitchen, he said, "Rasamah, tomorrow is the day we will go to the restaurant. We will go to a Chinese restaurant so you can try something other than chicken soup and porridge."

The next day, Rasamah polished Kandasamy's best shoes until they sparkled. She pressed a new white shirt and his beige trousers until the creases stood out like a knife's edge. She laid them out on the bed with clean socks and underclothes. She looked through her own wardrobe, trying to decide on what to wear. At festivals and weddings, who was better dressed than the wife of Mr Kandasamy?

For once, Kandasamy returned to the house at 6pm sharp. By the time he had showered and changed, Rasamah was pinning up her hair with the white jasmine flowers Kandasamy had brought in from the garden. At 6.30pm, a car horn outside announced that the evening was to start in style with a taxi ride to the restaurant. As they sat close to each other in the taxi, Rasamah inhaled the scent of his Yardley powder, which she remembered from the first time she sat beside him on the manavarai. When the taxi drove through Mountbatten Road, she looked out at Robinsons, Whiteaways and John Little. She told Kandasamy that she once thought of buying imported bedsheets from these shops.

"If I can't visit foreign countries, I thought I could bring a little of those countries into our home," Rasamah said to Kandasamy.

She asked Kandasamy how he knew about this restaurant. Kandasamy replied that the staff had given Mr Gould a congratulatory dinner there when he was awarded a medal for shooting a crocodile that had crawled up the bank of the Klang River.

"I hope they don't serve us any crocodile meat here." She glanced up at her husband holding open the swing door for her to enter.

Kandasamy ordered enough dishes to cover the table; fish, chicken and vegetables but no red meat because, he told Rasamah, you never knew what it might be, perhaps even crocodile. Rasamah covered her mouth but laughed aloud at her husband's joke, happy in her heart that Kandasamy was at last so relaxed that he was joking with her.

Kandasamy looked into her smiling face. "Your waiting for me at home with your tasty food and smiling face makes me forget all my problems, Rasamah."

Rasamah leaned forward, squeezing Kandasamy's arm. When he clasped her fingers firmly in his, she recalled feeling that same touch on their wedding day, when Amma had taken her hand and rested it in his.

Kandasamy guided her into the shop with the biggest "Giant Reduction" sign. The sarees were piled high, their infinite colours and designs shimmering in the light. Kandasamy went outside the shop to smoke his evening cheroot while Rasamah looked through the piles of material. She looked down at her own mauve silk saree embroidered with small red rosebuds. She looked back at the sarees and chose one she thought Chelvi would like.

"Athan, can we buy this for Chelvi?"

"Why? What is the occasion?" Kandasamy smiled.

"None. Just that I am so lucky that she is my dear friend. She is always there for me."

As she got back into the taxi, Rasamah leant over and kissed Kandasamy lightly on the cheek. She sat quietly close to him on the way home and blushed when she remembered all her grumbles to Chelvi. The light from the street made bars of light and shade fall across Kandasamy's face.

Rasamah's hope for change didn't last very long. The next night, Kandasamy came home later than usual. He was not carrying a bundle of files but a pint bottle. He sat in his usual chair and slammed the bottle onto the side table beside it. Rasamah tapped her chest, sensing a whiff of trouble in the air. He pulled the stopper open and threw it on the floor. The bottle toppled over. She brought it upright, but the foamy liquid streamed over the table. Rasamah read "ginger beer" on the label of the bottle.

"Athan, is your stomach troubling you? Or any bad news you heard?"

He glared at her, his forehead turning darker. His moustache curved even lower. Kandasamy refused to reply but opened his daily paper and shook the pages as if they were boys he had caught raiding their papaya trees. Folding the paper, he threw it across the table, where it fell in a disordered pile on the floor. Thumping his palm on his forehead, he ground his teeth, hit his head on the wall and cursed to himself in Tamil. She had never seen her husband's temper as bad as this.

Rasamah went to fetch a cloth to mop up the spilt drink. She let the cold water from the tap run over her shaking hands as she rinsed the cloth. She saw him walking to the study and joined him there.

"Your breaking the secret about my promotion was a cruel joke. Chellapah congratulated me and told the whole office. When I asked him how he knew this secret, he said that you had told Chelvi."

"Oh Kadavulai, I shared your good news with my only friend and sole companion. Without her, I am all alone in this house from morning till night." Rasamah began to chant prayers beneath her breath, hoping Kandasamy would calm down, but his voice rose higher and louder.

"When the whole office heard prematurely about my promotion, my boss was forced to cancel it. He had planned it as a fait accompli 'instruction' from his boss to promote me above my seniors before they could protest." He threw his inkpot against the wall. Black ink on white paint. Droplets landed on her skin.

"Athan, I am so very sorry. Please forgive me. I too dreamt of your promotion. Not in my worst nightmares did I know that my innocent word to Chelvi would force its cancellation." Her palms were cold.

"Talk about cooking, your garden or the temple but not my office secrets!" Kandasamy yelled as he hit his knuckles against his forehead.

Her mouth was parched. The air around her tasted bitter. She fell silent. He shook his study table until it rattled. A vase fell to the floor and broke. Some of the shards pricked her bare feet.

Where, Rasamah thought, *is Lord Ganesha? Now I need protection.* Rasamah remembered how pleased Chelvi had been when she had given her the present of the saree, yet that same Chelvi had betrayed her to the husband who beat her. Chelvi had promised faithfully that she would tell no one of Rasamah's news, yet she had used Rasamah's secret to get in her husband's good books; in turn, he had used her secret to show off in front of his colleagues and humiliate her husband.

"Think long before you speak. This is not our old village."

"Athan, you loved me because I spoke my mind freely."

"That doesn't include revealing my office secrets and destroying my chance of a promotion!" The lines on his face cut in deeper.

"In Karai Nagar, I leant forwards to hear whatever you promised me. In Malaya, you force me to shut my ears. But Athan, not once have you taken me outside Kuala Lumpur."

"Don't change the subject." Kandasamy stared at her.

She rubbed her temples. The masala she scraped off the grinding stone earlier for the mutton curry made her nauseous.

"You have brought this on yourself. You have ruined our chance to go anywhere," he said.

"I accepted your marriage proposal because I wanted to see Malaya and visit other places."

"Then you should have married the doctor your mother wanted to arrange for you." Kandasamy's voice became icy.

Rasamah's stomach churned; she dashed to the bathroom. Pulling the towel from the rack, she wiped her face. The roughness of the towel mocked her. She flung it outside the bathroom door and it fell at Kandasamy's feet. She saw him kicking it before he walked out through the back door. She ran behind him. He was already a few metres away, and she caught a glimpse of him passing the rain tree. She called after him but not once did he turn his head. Running back into the bedroom, she pulled her suitcase from beneath her bed. She took from it all the pictures of places she had hoped to visit and tore them into strips. Then, fumbling among the bedsheets and sarees in the wardrobe, she pulled out her application for teaching and tore that into shreds.

The fan in the corner of the bedroom scattered the fragments of paper around the floor. Rasamah turned the fan off and sat down, feeling defeated.

Much later, her puffed-up eyes scanned the scattered images of cobblestones and tiny bits with "Ire...cation... Conv..." She turned to look at the deities placed in an alcove where chinks of light came through. She stood up, wrapping her saree shawl over her shoulders. Minutes later she went into the kitchen, removed that morning's newspaper and spread it open as a backing to glue the pictures back together. She gathered up all the destroyed pieces to assemble them like puzzle pieces. Tears bit the corners of her eyes again; she knew it was impossible to patch the application letter back. She collected the shreds, rolled them into a ball and pressed it close to her chest for a moment before throwing it outside her bedroom window.

Rasamah saw Kandasamy leaving for work. She willed him to look back at her, an indication of his willingness to resolve their fight.

She stepped down from the house to pick hibiscus and jasmine buds while she listened to the chatter of the magpies. "So it is you," she called out to them, "all dressed up in black and white for a night at the opera." She turned around when she heard a sound behind her. It was Chelvi coming up the garden path with a tray of kesari. The sight of her friend caused Rasamah to spill all her gathered flowers.

"What happened? Mr Chellapah telling Mr Kandasamy didn't get promotion."

Rasamah ran towards Chelvi and shook her. "I shared the secret of my Athan's promotion with you. You betrayed me and told your husband who blabbed it to the whole office. Amma warned me that I am too unsuspecting and trusting." She pushed Chelvi back through the gate and replaced the latch. She could hear Chelvi crying. "Acca, when anybody beat me, you said you would protect me, that you can be my teacher..."

"It is you who have taught me a lesson today."

That afternoon, Rasamah fetched the clothes from the line, only to drop them to the ground when she spotted a magpie with a broken wing. She picked it up and stroked it before she wrapped it up in one of Kandasamy's clean cotton singlets. While she began to nurse it, she pictured Chelvi's gaunt face; her thin, sparse hairline. She looked at the bird.

Since I have lost my only friend, I have just you to talk to, without your beak blabbing. I fear that Chellapah may have threatened to choke Chelvi to death if she didn't reveal any secrets to help him compete with my Athan. She was the first one to greet me so warmly when I arrived in Kuala Lumpur. Isn't the first cut the deepest? Even if we bleed from it we keep coming back for more. She needed protection from her alcoholic and violent husband while I craved companionship because of my workaholic Athan.

I can heal your broken wing...and I know that Chelvi will return. When she does, shall I forgive her to heal both her wing and mine?

DODOL FOR
THE DOCTOR

SCOTT ROAD, BRICKFIELDS, KUALA LUMPUR

Rasamah Kandasamy had such "hot, hot" news to tell Chelvi that her lips began to burn. For the third time, she peered out of her kitchen window but saw only mynahs pecking on her clusters of cream-coloured moringa buds. *Ah, finally, here comes Chelvi through my back gate.* When Rasamah unlocked the door, she saw the tail of Chelvi's saree brushing the mynahs aside as she picked the moringa buds for herself.

It was a special day after all, and she had to celebrate the great news. In one small, warming pot of ghee, she roasted a cupful of cashew nuts and raisins "until golden" to complement her dodol. She recalled Chelvi buying similar ingredients three days ago when they were at the sundry shop; the shopkeeper jotted down her debt onto the yellow 555-brand credit notebook. That time she hadn't offered to pay for Chelvi. She laid out the ingredients on the old newspaper spread out on her outer veranda and started to light a firewood stove.

"Tortoises are never my friends," Rasamah called through the window.

"Sorry, Acca, I giving up after-lunch juicy sleep to come and help my best friend."

"You can make up for all your sins by helping me to make this dodol."

"Are you celebrating, you make this sweet, Acca?"

"Yes, and I want to be especially kind to Kandasamy in case something terrible happens to me."

"What is this, Acca? Celebrate something terrible? What frightening thing our astrologer told you?" Chelvi rubbed the sweat off her face on her blouse sleeve.

"No 'horror-scope' horror." Rasamah shook her head. "Kandasamy told me his death sentence was only one month away. On the 31st, the heavens fall."

"Who is going to kill him?"

"Your Chellapah would, if he could."

"Aiyo, he's not so bad."

"This year I turn forty-five, my Kamala matures to twenty but sadly my Athan turns fifty-five."

"Why is Mr Kandasamy's birthday a sad time?"

"It's my Athan's compulsory retirement date. When we first came here and Kandasamy worked all day long in his office, I was so lonely. But after all these years, I'm used to having the house to myself. I have no idea what it will be like to have both of us here all the time. Now, evenings, Kandasamy is in his study. Saturday, I do shopping. Sunday, Kandasamy has all the newspapers. But, oh Lord Ganesha, every day! And no work, no files, no letters. He will be like a jungle tiger prowling around looking for his dinner. Although this tiger eats paper, he is no paper tiger. So I make him his favourite sweet."

"You can't invite me to your house like before?" Chelvi's betel-stained teeth bit her lower lip.

"Is your Chellapah competing with my Kandasamy to clear his files? I hear that his retirement date is also drawing near."

"I don't know about Mr Chellapah's plans."

"Don't tell me you and your husband didn't notice Mr Kandasamy carry the office files pressed to his chin while making sure not to trip over the roots sprouting from the angsana trees?"

"No, Acca, but I know that my Chellapah complains, so much work to clear." Rasamah watched how Chelvi's arms widened as if expanding the bellows on an accordion.

"Both of us are going to be stuck with retired husbands at home all day. I have to be content with the four walls of my kitchen cell. Kandasamy will be busy looking up and down the four edges of the newspapers instead of us going to Ireland and Amma-land. If Amma hears, she would ask what four people would say if they heard. I have been worrying about all these."

"You are not a worrier?"

"No, not a worrier and I don't want to be taken for granted or become a forest donkey eaten by a tiger with no files to read. Once my Athan is divorced…"

"Aiyo, why talking divorce? *Sial*." Chelvi rotated the ring on her finger.

"Not from me but from his office. Aiyo, help me get my mind off these forest things with some cooking and I can tell you the celebration news that is already boiling over inside of me." Rasamah took out one large wooden paddle along with two scraper spoons and closed the drawer. She walked past Chelvi, who was by now leaning against the kitchen pillar, and gave Chelvi's saree shawl a flip. "Lord Ganesha gave us a great blessing," Rasamah called out.

Rasamah noted how Chelvi snuck her hand back to wrap her synthetic silk saree shawl around her waistline. Chelvi's eyes met hers, registering Rasamah's excitement, then wandered over to the ingredients Rasamah had laid out on old newspaper on the outer veranda and the firewood stove Rasamah had started over an hour ago, which sputtered.

"Acca, tell lah, why you so excited? What blessing *he* gave?"

"Kamala has received a marriage proposal."

Emboldened, Chelvi snapped the stems off each of the six moringa pods she had picked. She paused a little longer, then said, "Why beating drums for daytime-coming proposals?"

Annoyed now, Rasamah said, "I see you are selecting not only the drumsticks from my murungakkai tree but also the precious buds. This proposal is not from any fellow on the street."

At Rasamah's mention of the buds, Chelvi looked guilty. Small leaves had become entangled in Chelvi's hair bun, thinned from her husband's constant pulling at it. Rasamah sighed and removed the leaves one by one. "It was from someone in a hospital."

"Oh, what sickness is he suffering from?"

"Lovesickness."

"Nowdays hospital can cure that?" Chelvi asked.

"Eh, silly bodoh, he is not a patient. Here, help me while I cook. Hold this tumbler for me to measure. Two pounds of pulut flour."

"You mean two elbees?"

Rasamah positioned a wrought-iron pot over the wood fire and splashed cold water on it to test the heat before pouring the ingredients into it.

Chelvi asked Rasamah why she preferred cooking over firewood when she had a new Butterfly-brand stove sitting on a concrete slab in her kitchen. Rasamah swung a buri-palm leaf in her face, asking if she had forgotten how the wood fire greatly enhanced the taste of curries and desserts. To keep the flame going strong Rasamah handed Chelvi the fan, but Chelvi's fervent fanning made sparks fly out. Some landed on Rasamah's foot but she shook them off.

"Kadavulai! Chelvi, why you aim your fire arrows on my metti?" Her toes smarted from the sparks. Chelvi was still careless even after all her teaching.

"Aiyo, sorry, Acca." Chelvi stumbled off the stool.

"This is not how you make my marriage glow again." On her wedding day, Kandasamy had "sealed his love" by slipping a pair of thin silver rings on each of her second toes. Rasamah snatched the fan from her friend. "Go bring the bottle of gingelly oil from my storeroom. You know where it is." As Chelvi scurried off, Rasamah rubbed her ear, feeling like she heard a chuckle.

After dripping a couple of drops of the oil onto the blisters, the two friends began to put the ingredients together in the pot and get it going.

Finally, Chelvi said, "So this proposal from hospital attendant or what?"

Rasamah continued to stir the mixture to avoid lumps from forming. "Try higher, my curious cat."

"Kadavulai, my God, Kamala got proposal from a doctor?" Chelvi cupped her mouth.

"Correct."

"Acca, unmarried doctors get many proposals, not send any? More fishiness here than in the fish stall in our market." Chelvi rocked on her feet as she sat.

"You remember last month my Kamala received an invitation to play her violin at a concert to be broadcast on Radio Malaya?"

"Yes, so lucky, that teacher knows people in the radio station and so introduced her lah."

"Not luck," Rasamah raised her eyebrows. "Kamala is her teacher's best student and her teacher is the best in KL. That is why we chose him. So not luck if Radio Malaya asks for recommendations. If your husband didn't spend all his money on beer, maybe your daughter could have had music lessons too."

Chelvi's eyes focused on the steam rising from the pot.

Rasamah stirred and blended the simmering dodol with ferocity until it began turning into a whirlpool of gold. "Anyway, this doctor was at the concert with his parents and when the performance finished, he made straight for my Kamala. Myself, I'm not surprised, as my Kamala was wearing her best saree and she had left her glasses at home especially for the concert. So, when the doctor boy caught a glimpse of Kamala's green mata kuching eyes, it was he who was caught. And his eyes could look nowhere else."

Chelvi swept her fingers over her eyes, saying they were smarting from the smoke. Rasamah struck the ladle on the edge of the pot to shake down the gooey delicacy. The cast iron going *tung, tung, tung* got Chelvi's attention. Rasamah continued, "He asked his mother and father to introduce him to Kandasamy, Kamala and me, so that he could congratulate us on having such a talented daughter."

"Aiyo, so polite this boy, not like the girl's mother, ya?"

"You don't be rude. No rambutan or langsat for you. And no apples for me."

"Why Acca?"

"'Because an apple a day keeps the doctor away and I want this doctor to come our way."

"So, share, share. What happened next?"

"Kandasamy and I met with his parents last night. They wanted to know if Kamala's horoscope is a match. And that is big, big news."

Chelvi suddenly plunged her spoon into the pot of dodol. Some splashed over the side.

Rasamah jolted. "Hey, jumping frogs, I know, but not jumping dodol. How many times I tell you to be careful?"

Contrite, Chelvi returned to the low wooden stool and helped Rasamah stir the bubbling dodol. The mixture thickened. Chelvi gripped the centre of the ladle with both hands. The fragrance of caramelised sugar and pandan leaves wafted over the veranda, passing through the kitchen before filling the whole house with its aroma. Seeing Chelvi inhale, Rasamah smiled, reminded of the time her classmates performed *Macbeth* at the final-year concert in the convent decades ago. The dodol was coming out perfectly for the doctor.

"Can you keep this secret? Or will you let Chellapah choke it out of you?" Rasamah extended her right palm for Chelvi to place hers on top.

Chelvi put up her greasy palms peppered with ash from the burning logs. "Acca, I don't want to dirty your hands."

Chelvi being thoughtful for once.

"So what you want to do about this big horoscope problem you have?"

"I have you to help me, so I'm sure there is no problem." One thing Rasamah could say for Chelvi: she was happy to be at Rasamah's beck and call. "Tomorrow carry three extra coconuts to break for crushing all obstacles in Kamala's way before matching the doctor boy's horoscope with hers. Doctor boy's parents want to see Kamala's horoscope first before proposal is official."

The dodol was almost done. But then, Chelvi's words stopped her in her tracks. "Kamala so lucky girl," said Chelvi, "but Acca, maybe this doctor... Sorry, sorry Acca, so sorry, forgive me to say, maybe doctor boy not free."

"Eh, don't give sour news when preparing sweets; I don't want my delicacy to smell like burnt coffee seeds." Rasamah got up to wipe her glasses with the edge of her saree; her vision blurred with the moisture in her eyes. But did she hear correctly that Chelvi muttered under her breath, "At last can rest lah"?

Rasamah scooped up two portions of dodol to pack for Chelvi. When Chelvi asked if Rasamah could add an extra scoop to reserve for her daughter, who would return from outstation that weekend, Rasamah topped that portion up, knowing Chelvi was so deprived, and said that Chellapah should not have even a pinch of it.

Ah, that woman and her "not-free boy". How can I find out? I know, all these doctors know each other and there's Athan's relative Dr Muthurajah. For sure, the doctor cousin will know the boy's family, and I remember how fond Dr Muthurajah is of dodol, so perhaps a little visit is due.

In the rickshaw on the way home Rasamah congratulated herself for a successful afternoon. The Muthurajahs did indeed know the family and there were two elder sisters, both married— to doctors. Rasamah was pleased with her ploy in finding out so quickly whether her daughter had a proper suitor and the successful outcome of her questioning, she could not resist stopping off at Chelvi's house to tell her the good news and, at the same time, collect the glass Pyrex dish she had allowed Chelvi to borrow to take home some of the dodol they had cooked together.

The next day was Friday.

Saras, Dr Selladurai's nurse, rang to say, "One Mrs Chellapah came in complaining of chest pains. As the doctor placed his stethoscope on her chest, she showed him a photo of her daughter. Mrs Chellapah also gave him a package."

Rasamah struggled to understand what Saras was saying. It took her a few moments. "There is more than one Mrs Chellapah in our community." Rasamah slowly placed the receiver down.

By 2.30pm, Rasamah had polished a tray and placed on it a comb of ripe rastali bananas, a box of camphor and kumkuma in a bronze holder.

Chelvi came over to sit next to Rasamah.

"Aiyo, I planning to leave after the first part of pooja is over."

"Oh why?" Rasamah shook the orange-handled fabric bag that she used at the temple until the dust flew into Chelvi's face, before putting three coconuts inside.

Chelvi rubbed her eyes.

"I'm taking medicines." Chelvi showed her a tiny brown packet.

"Why your eyes twitching even more if the doctor had checked your heart?"

"The drops burning my eyes, Acca."

The kettle was on the stove. Rasamah wove pieces of string between her fingers, forming patterns of jasmine flowers and buds, yellow marigolds with red hibiscus, two centimetres apart. As she corrected Chelvi on how to tie the ends of each garland, Rasamah casually asked, "Did you visit Dr Selladurai and show him a picture?"

Chelvi's face turned reddish-brown. She quickly got up to clear the table. In her panic, Chelvi broke a Noritake saucer. Rasamah jumped at the sound of crashing china.

"Acca, I feel bit nervous today. Maybe ashamed about how my husband beats me all the time, not giving me money. But you already know, so it's okay, Acca."

Rasamah pondered her friend's face for a few seconds. "I have learnt many things about you, Chelvi."

"Like what, Acca?" Chelvi bundled the garlands into a piece of damp cloth.

Rasamah had gone back and forth in her mind about what to do with Chelvi. She had still been of two minds even as the sound of crashing china reached her, but for her desperate lone-liness and the sake of their friendship Rasamah felt compelled to make this trip offer, almost as if she owed it to Chelvi and herself. Measuredly, she spoke, "I will tell you during our big poitu varain to Penang and return to Kuala Lumpur. Don't you want a short holiday on our own?"

Rasamah told Chelvi about how she often tantalised herself with images of the two of them exploring Penang together, eating the fried kuay teow, mee mamak and Penang rojak to their hearts' content.

Chelvi asked about visiting temples and shopping.

Rasamah replied that not only would they visit all the Hindu temples but also see the famous Snake Temple that Mrs Chong raved about. They would lounge by Batu Ferringhi beach, the two of them, wearing big sunglasses and sipping juice from fresh coconuts, attracting all manner of stares…oh, that would be like a movie-star life… Mother Superior and Amma might for once agree that they were so happy for her.

Chelvi looked scared. "A short trip, Acca? Husband won't have anybody to cook for him."

"Just three days without us at home. Let us teach them to appreciate us at last," said Rasamah.

Chelvi's eyes darted to Rasamah's face, and then to the dustpan and broom she was using to clean up the broken shards. "My husband may beat me some more if I try to run away."

"He can't beat you while you are away with me."

Rasamah powdered her face and joined Chelvi.

Rasamah put moringa buds that she had plucked herself on Chelvi's hair bun.

"Come, carry your bag and stop dreaming…"

As agreed, they set off for the Kandaswamy temple towards the lower end of Scott Road. Since they were in a hurry, the five-minute walk took her just three this evening. The temple, a miniature replica of the Nallur Kandaswamy Kovil in Jaffna, was situated on the road where she lived; it was very close to Rasamah's heart. Since it was the first Friday of the month, the flower sellers' carts were heaped with garlands of chrysanthemum and red roses alongside their usual fare of jasmines and marigolds, but nothing could compare to the design she had woven with Chelvi for this Friday's pooja.

She had always admired the way Chelvi wove the buds for special garlands for the gods.

"Have you finished your packing?"

"What are you planning, Acca?" Chelvi asked.

Rasamah stood at the bend where coconut shells were discarded and the coconut water left tiny streams on the path of sand near the whitewashed walls. Rays shining through the carved statues glittered on the scallops of their offering trays, reflecting onto Rasamah's gold bangles. The jewellery that she owned would only weigh her down, she decided. She closed her eyes to picture herself back in the Nallur Kandaswamy Temple in Ceylon, where her Amma had taken her on feast days. All the hopes she had had then. Teaching at a school and travelling outside Kuala Lumpur. It all seemed a lifetime ago.

"Acca, you look like a Cantonese opera star," said Chelvi. "Extra powder on your face, Acca. Let me wipe." Using her handkerchief, Chelvi dabbed at Rasamah's cheeks.

Right then and there, Rasamah decided. "We will go away to Penang for three days." Chelvi hesitated, looking uncertain.

Rasamah urged, "I must because once Kamala gets married and my Athan retires, I will be caged in my kitchen on permanent home duty. Come, let's make our prayers. I will ask Lord Shiva Om Pinakine Namaha to guard the path of dharma so that both our families will be safe always."

Rasamah gathered a handful of fresh hibiscus flowers as she approached the main altar and bowed before individual deities in whitewashed altars. The corridor was lit by her favourite shell-shaped oil lamps. It was already full of worshippers. The husks on Rasamah's overflowing offering tray caught on the saree shawls of some worshippers, prompting the ones in front to nudge one another aside.

The temple bell rose to loud chimes at the end of the prayer. The bright yellow veil, looped with red nylon string, that covered the deity was scrolled back by the priests' assistant, revealing Lord Shiva. Rasamah raised her tray, laden with rolled bunches of jasmine buds, hibiscus, banana combs and coconuts, for blessing. "Oh Lord Shiva...guide us towards our mothers and our customs. Om Shambhave Namaha." Rasamah finished chanting her prayer and then opened her eyes. Chelvi was standing in front of the altar with her own offering of two coconuts and a flower garland. In all the years she had known Chelvi, Rasamah had never seen her approach the altar before Rasamah finished her prayers.

"I also pray for daughters," Chelvi whispered. "Daughters must follow mothers' advice and have good lives."

Rasamah nodded. "Thank you, Chelvi. You are a good friend, and as a special treat, we will go to eat nice cool ice cream before we go home."

As Chelvi stepped down, Rasamah noticed that Chelvi wore her slippers on the wrong feet and told her that after prayers, she should not be thinking upside down any more.

Rasamah hoped that the green rice-flour jelly of the chendol strips would cool down Chelvi's fears of taking a holiday away from her husband. Rasamah took comfort in the thought that no matter the time or the weather, Chelvi would accompany her during the festive sale. Chelvi had never said no to any of her requests. As she thought of Chelvi hiding impishly behind two new pillows—"buy one free one"—Rasamah concealed a smile. Most of all, she felt pride seeing her "student" mingling without fear with the women at the temple committee, some of them the wives of doctors. Because of Chelvi, she now had two more requests for English tuition classes for their children. That Chellapah was the evil one who influenced her to cheat, lie and steal. No wonder my cutlery drawer has more forks than their matching spoons.

"I like you and I hate you at the same time." Rasamah stroked Chelvi's arm.

Chelvi caught her breath slurping the last spoonful of the cold dessert.

Despite the cold, welcome taste of chendol ice cream, which cooled them both, walking in the hot late-afternoon sun made perspiration trickle down their foreheads afterwards.

"Ah, so hot," Rasamah remarked, "let's take a rickshaw."

"Or let me give you both a lift in my car," said a voice behind them.

Rasamah and Chelvi turned quickly to see who their benefactor might be.

"Why, Doctor Selladurai." The pleasure in Rasamah's voice was apparent. She looked up at Dr Selladurai's wavy hair, a neat parting on the side, while Chelvi hid behind her. "Chelvi, this is the doctor I mentioned to you who was so fond of my Kamala's violin playing."

"Hello, Mrs Kandasamy," said the doctor, bowing slightly, "and Mrs Chellapah."

Rasamah looked at Chelvi.

"I hope you are not having any more chest pains, Mrs Chellapah," Dr Selladurai continued. "Your heart rate is normal and you have nothing to worry about."

Rasamah turned to Chelvi, "Your heart? I thought you had a problem with your eyes?"

"Yes, yes…" The sweat ran heavily down Chelvi's forehead. "Heart first, then eyes. Come, come, I am late to get home."

Dr Selladurai looked closer at Chelvi. "If your delightful daughter is home when you get there, please tell her how much I enjoyed the dodol you gave me. She must be a very clever cook. The dodol was indeed delicious. From the picture you showed me, she is a most attractive girl. Her husband will be a fortunate man."

A noise rang out like a temple gong as Rasamah dropped the bag carrying the brass offering tray on the hot, hot pavement on Scott Road.

FLOWERS
FOR KK

I have been dying inside for eight years. Yet, my three-quarters-dead body is sitting at the funeral of my late husband. I am using my handkerchief not to wipe away my tears but to hide how few I have left. Almost all of them have been used up in my eight years of marriage. Another woman beside me is wailing away. I feel twice betrayed, first by my late husband, Kanagaretnam, alias King Kana or KK to family and friends, and second by my younger sister, Thangachi. Whose treachery was worse?

The temple priest places camphor and sandalwood-perfumed incense sticks in an antique copper incense holder. Then, on a large silver tray strewn with white jasmine and red rose petals, he sprinkles rosewater. He gestures to Thangachi to place this at the foot of the dark-brown, gold-lined timber coffin. The wind blows smoke from the lit incense sticks. Grey ash flies to land on the green-and-white mosaic floor. Some fall and cling on to Thangachi's hands, wet with her many tears. The fragrance of the flowers, especially the sweet scent of frangipani and white jasmine from the wreaths, pervades the house. Thangachi continues weeping.

There are many tributes, from words to flowers, from the relatives, friends, colleagues and staff of King Kana. A tall young man says, "Mrs Kana, Chief KK helped to arrange a housing loan for my first home. I will always be grateful to him."

I hear two older men standing opposite me agreeing with each other as to what a capable man he was. One mentions that he was so strict that his finance division shone as the most disciplined and efficient department in all of the country. Another says the department had won several best-service awards because of King Kana. I shake my head thinking, if they only knew what I have gone through, they might not think he is as good a man as all that. Among the difficult things about life with KK was accompanying him to official dinners, weddings or even to our temple on Fridays. All dressed up, KK would fling our bedroom door wide open before I was ready, place his heavy wooden armchair at the entrance, sit cross-legged and make me turn around so he could check whether I had evenly layered the talcum powder on my face and neck. His precise instructions had to be perfectly carried out. "Kondai, neatly clasped in black hairpin and black hair net, without any strand of stray hair jutting out, kondai placed not too high, slightly low almost touching the back just above your choli saree blouse."

As soon as our relatives and friends leave, I will have more than a word with Thangachi.

Om namo namo namo

Om namo namo namo

Om namo namo namo…

It had been sung at Papa's funeral. How I wept. One second our Papa was there and the next he was gone. "Our Papa is no more," I sobbed. My psychologist friend says that my wailing at Papa's funeral had a very useful purpose. My pent-up emotions and grief were released in one go. If the steam from the boiling kettle were not allowed a spout to escape, it may explode later. Here, beside King Kana's corpse, I retreat even deeper into my mute mode than when he had been alive. Since I am too numb and stunned to weep, will I explode later? *Thangachi watch out*, I say to myself.

I lower my handkerchief to stare at Thangachi. I recall the November evening of dark clouds and thunder a year ago, when King Kana pointed his forefinger as he told me, "Indra, you have been childless for so long."

He said "you", not "we". I had just served him his evening Ceylon tea, strong with freshly boiled milk and one teaspoon of honey, accompanied with kolukattai. KK demanded that every cup of tea be served with one sweet delicacy, the way his mother used to serve his father and him. That evening, we were both seated in the sitting room. He spread out on the sofa, his arms resting on his favourite "Made in England" lily-white linen cushion from Robinsons, and I on my brown rattan chair with my self-embroidered beige cushion.

"I must do something." He jabbed the cushion.

Now it was "I", not "you" or "we". It was him or me; him against me.

"You know our custom."

"Which one?" I folded my arms.

"You know, the one where the husband marries the childless wife's single sister."

"Oh, that one." I was deliberately casual. "I thought the wife had to die first before the husband remarried?"

Only the previous evening, when I was standing at my bedroom window admiring the thick pink-and-white bougainvillea bushes, I overheard KK talking to Thangachi in the garden on one of her many visits. He mentioned something about a date between the seventh and tenth of December as a good time for marriages, according to our Hindu calendar. Silly me; I had thought Thangachi was going to surprise me with some good news. I moved behind the curtain so as not to be spotted.

Back in the sitting room, he hit our wooden table with his clenched fist, making the teaspoons jump and clatter on the saucer.

I felt a low punch to my stomach.

"Not necessarily," he continued later with gritted teeth. "If she has not been productive for many years that's some kind of death. It's your duty to bear children."

"So, are you planning to proceed as if I am presumed dead?" I asked. Sarcasm gave me some consolation.

He wagged his forefinger. "From Alaska to Bhutan to China and India, from the Apache to the Sioux Red Indians to the Swazi in Africa, they have been practising these, what they call soror...something. Oh yes, sororate marriages. Why should we in Malaya stick out as ignorant exceptions?" It seemed he had been preparing his arguments for this.

He didn't know that after overhearing him discuss his plans with Thangachi, I had gone to the same library while he was at the club later that afternoon. The library assistant said she hadn't had time to replace the reference books that KK had pored over. I collapsed on the same chair he had sat on earlier, perspiring despite the ceiling fan beating the air at maximum speed. I jumped with joy to read that the same books also said that the Hindu Bania caste practised what were called levirate as compared to sororate marriages.

As I read, I was reminded that this lover of things English had forgotten that the Irish nuns in our convent had taught me that when Arthur, Prince of Wales, died, his widow, Catherine of Aragon, married his younger brother, the future Henry VIII. When Prince Albert died, his fiancée Mary married his younger brother, the future George V. I could well imagine how KK would react if I reminded him of all this, so I decided yet again that I was better off keeping dumb voluntarily and saving whatever was left of my dissipating dignity.

KK flung his cup of hot tea against the showcase where our wedding portrait and other photos were displayed. Raising his voice, which he did whenever his argument was weak, he said, "It's your fault that I have to marry Thangachi. She should bring hope, like our sacred lotus filled with fertility, to overcome your bad karma!"

I wiped the splashes of tea from our wedding portrait. I saw myself as a smiling bride seven years ago, a bride with large eyes and black wavy hair pinned with white jasmine, with a glow of much hope all over my face.

"We are keeping it within the family," KK said, as he noticed my reddened eyes.

I had wanted to ask whether all the world's darkest secrets weren't kept within families. Aren't most wounds caused by ourselves or within families? My kolukattai had bypassed his heart to reach his stomach, which he was stroking. I had caught him more than once pretending to stroke his tummy, as he felt that it was manlier to show prosperity instead of chest pain.

The malligai in my vase had wilted. The dark clouds outside were followed by lightning, thunder and rain. I recall something that Thangachi had said. I was cooking KK's dinner one evening when KK decided that he was a free bachelor once again and that I no longer existed. Thangachi had joined me in the kitchen without being invited, asserting among other things her traditional rights as my sister. Out of nowhere, she had said to me, "Remember our unlucky aunty, PPP, Poor Pitiful Punitham? They called her that because her first bed was barren. Her husband married her sister, who produced two kids from the second bed."

In the early days when it was just Thangachi, Amma, Papa and me, Amma still did all the cooking at home although we were both teenagers, as she loved preparing all our favourite foods.

The kitchen was her queendom and I felt like an intruder. Because Amma had marked her territory firmly, I told Thangachi that we should retreat into branches of domestic science that did not overlap with Amma's. I became busy with sewing, embroidery and an area of cooking—namely, cake making—that required my use of the kitchen only for short and off-peak periods.

I made what Amma said was the best kolukattai. I also baked cakes in various shapes and colours as elaborate as my embroidery. As a Libran, I had chosen harmony and peace over conflict. However, Thangachi had said, "Acca, unlike you, I will advance. Why can't we have two tigresses in our kitchen mountain since the older one looks tired lately?"

She had done so, staying in the kitchen not only whenever Amma was out of it but whenever Amma was too busy to notice. Yes, Thangachi, with her childlike smile, was aggressive and impatient—such a contrast to me. She would be ideal for any young ambitious man, so I couldn't understand why she would be happy to barge into my home to be a second wife to KK, whose good looks could not overshadow his dark and violent side.

When Papa brought home bangles and other nice things for us, Amma and I had the first choice before Thangachi took her turn. "I know you are Papa's favourite," she had said to me.

"I only happen to be older than you, that's all." I gave her all the bangles Papa had given me, but she continued to sulk. I wondered why she had brought this up, and as I paused at the stove, Thangachi took the wooden cooking spoon from my hand and carried on with preparing the meal I had been cooking, as if it were the most natural thing in the world. As the weight of what she was saying sank in, I sat down on the nearest chair. Of course, I knew that it was taking a long time for us to have our first child but I had hoped...it would never happen to me. "Oh Lord Ganesha, let me never be the one to be accused of sleeping on a barren bed," I prayed. Yet now my worst fear had come true.

The very next day, KK made it clear that he no longer considered me his sole wife, let alone his soulmate. We had planned to go together to a gala dinner at the Lake Club where KK was to be fêted. I yearned to wear the dark-green or the deep-magenta sarees that Papa had bought me years ago, but KK said that those colours hurt his eyes. He insisted I wear one of the pastel ones that he had got for me. The border of my saree hem should sit just above the floor, neither sweeping it nor resting too high above my sandals. Whenever his rules were not met, KK would make me untie my saree and do it all over again.

When I took too much time getting dressed, he drove off, leaving me stupefied and gaping. Thangachi, who was to come with us for the gala dinner and who should respect me as her elder sister, saw my humiliation.

She said, "Acca, small matter only, you have married such a handsome man who looks like my favourite Hollywood star, Tyrone Power. He is also wealthy, so what if he has a few faults?" Although she was younger than I, sometimes she seemed more worldly and wise.

Thus I was left behind with a sister who took my husband's side. I told Thangachi to go outside and find a taxi. I didn't trust KK to be on his own because he would be far from alone. All his lady friends would also be there, those European and Eurasian ladies with sleeveless and strapless blouses and God-knows-what-ever-else-less; Chinese ladies in tight cheongsams with high slits up the sides would all be sitting around the same dining table. Just as Thangachi and I arrived, I saw one of those boldly dressed women at our table. As Thangachi and I headed for the ladies' powder room, I deliberately let the long sequined mundhani of my saree sweep over that woman's face, hoping it might scrape off some of her make-up. Thangachi saw this and said she wasn't sure if I were more unhappy with KK or with that woman. I slammed the door.

Walking back to our table, Thangachi put her hand on my shoulder and said, "Acca, I can see you are angry. Don't you think you are blessed that our KK asked me to marry him?"

I had to admit to myself that Thangachi was right. KK could have stepped outside our custom and married someone from outside the family or even further away—one of those ladies from another race and religion. That new wife would have pushed me aside totally as we would have been strangers to each other; I would have had no influence at all on her, whereas Thangachi, who calls me Acca, would show me much more respect as KK's first wife and her elder sister, the way no alien could do.

Barely a month later, after having been a bride seven years before, I was leaning towards Thangachi to help her tie the pastel-blue wedding saree with golden embroidery that our late Amma had given me as my heirloom when I came of age.

I had arranged the mundhani so that the more intricate design from Amma's saree hung neatly over her shoulder. I consoled myself that if it weren't Thangachi but some other bride, I wouldn't even be allowed near the dressing room and the new bride wouldn't be wearing anything like a saree. Yet, I asked her, "Are you very sure you want to marry my husband?" My face was hollow and weary, and I felt that I was at a funeral not a wedding.

As I tried to place an equal number of matching blue and gold bangles on Thangachi's wrists, she squeezed my hands with her henna-stained fingers and said, "Acca, don't worry, I will always obey you both."

I heard KK reciting the same vows of fidelity, love and mutual respect which he had made when he led me seven times round the agni, the sacred fire of ghee and wooden sticks, seven years before. At the climax of the wedding ceremony, when KK tied the thali around Thangachi's neck, the accompanying mridangam and thavil drums, the Nadaswaram trumpets and temple bells, rose simultaneously to a crescendo, I was choking with shame.

KK went out of his way to prove that he had been right in marrying her while I was still alive. His gestures were so over-eager that they made him look clownish. He fasted, spread thicker strokes of vibhuti ash on his forehead and made special poojas to Lord Ganesha to remove the obstacles to his being a father. He raised his long arms to the temple ceiling, then prostrated himself with his hairy bare chest on the floor as he pleaded loudly with Lord Ganesha for just one chance. He offered the kolukattai that I had made for his pooja. I offered special poojas too with the softest, most evenly shaped extra kolukattai, as they are Lord Ganesha's favourites. Unlike KK, I did it secretly. I didn't want to lose what was left of my face if my prayers were ignored.

Within a month, something happened that none of the three of us could have imagined. First, I threw up. KK dismissed it as something I had eaten. As I settled on the sofa, Thangachi teased me, "Acca, I come into your family officially and so soon you are going to be a mother. I brought you luck."

Thangachi always took credit for all the good news in our family so this remark was nothing new to me, but I was happy to tell her that I had prayed to be a mother. At last, I was to be an Amma, the most precious word I knew. I smiled with each instance of Thangachi's continued self-praise.

Then, when Thangachi vomited two weeks later, KK congratulated her. "This is most welcome morning sickness." I wished I had thrown up on him. Our special poojas to Lord Ganesha had been answered more than once. He had prayed to be a father and got to be one, two times over.

Many a time, KK rushed home from work bringing with him piping hot vadai served with red-chilli and green-mint coconut chutney as well as sweet purple-yam porridge, showing how excited he was to have bought all that Thangachi craved for. KK brought some over to my room and I had to pretend not to notice they were cold leftovers from Thangachi's tea-time treat.

When my contractions began one morning, KK arranged for the driver to send me to the General Hospital to have my baby. I was in an empty double room. After I went into labour I saw my baby, Kumari, asleep and all wrapped up in a cot next to me; she had my thick wavy hair.

Four days later, KK rushed in to tell me that Thangachi had complained of pains and might be in early labour. He had brought her to the same hospital. Although the doctor had told him it was a false alarm, they decided to keep her in anyway so she stayed there. I just listened to what he said and saw how he had rushed off to see her. He spent more time by her bedside than mine. The nurses thought he was Thangachi's husband and merely my relative.

Barely a week after I had given birth to my baby, Kumari, Thangachi had hers. One of the nurses wheeled me into Thangachi's room, and I saw KK embracing Thangachi with enthusiasm, then lifting her baby, Raja, high in the air because he was a boy. Thangachi was the mother of a champ, so that made her a champ too. A baby daughter was clearly a runner-up. KK's late mother's heart-shaped emerald pendant and thick gold chain adorned Thangachi's now-fat neck at the hospital.

I was sent home with my baby first and had two quiet days with Kumari before Thangachi returned from the hospital, making her usual demands to KK in her shrill voice. "Please can you order sakkarai saddam, with extra brown sugar in the rice, crushed cardamom seeds and roasted cashew nuts sprinkled over it? Make sure you offer that as thanksgiving to Lord Ganesha for making you a father to our newborn son. After the blessing, bring a small portion back for both of us."

Unlike in past years, I saw a gentle smile on KK's face; his temper had disappeared, too. I saw him sitting on his usual sofa cooing to baby Raja.

Sometimes mothers die at childbirth, but this time it was the father who died of a heart attack within four weeks of our two babies being born. My friend, Mrs Chong, said "sei" in Cantonese meant both "four" and "death".

Now at the funeral, as the hearse pulls up at our main gate, Thangachi beats her head with both her palms. "Kadavulai, my God, why did you do this to him just when you have given us our greatest miracle? You have given me a son but you have taken away my husband."

She says "my", not "our" or "your", husband. When we were little girls, we loved playing pura-pura—pretend-pretend—games. All these months she has been pretending her life consisted only of herself, KK and her precious son. She wails for this man louder than I, showing his colleagues and friends that he means more to her than to her Acca. Our guests are slowly leaving. The white-and-yellow frangipani is fading. Outside, the sky is blue with white clouds. The sun is shining, too.

The last guest has left. I go to our sitting room and sit, spreading myself out on the sofa like KK used to. Thangachi follows me and sits on the rug. Her eyes follow me. Her cold fingertips touch my warm feet. And just as she reaches up to hug me, the moment I've been waiting for, I push her forehead back. Thangachi's eyes widen and her face becomes distorted. When she drops her jaw I see her lips are even more pale. She blinks as if to wake herself from this new nightmare. My mouth tightens.

"Too late for the old Acca business. Acca is dead, long live Amma. Now you have to pay me back."

"How, Amma? I have nothing to give."

"Nothing? Is your son nothing?"

"Aiyo, no, Amma." Thangachi starts to wail in a tone that's more genuinely frightened than her crescendo wailing for my husband earlier. "I'm so sorry, Amma. Aiyo, Amma! Please don't take my son. He's the only thing that I have."

"Well, you took all that I had."

Thangachi's sobs grow louder; maybe she won't even hear what I have to say next, my tone is so quiet. "To me, you are no different from the women of other races in the club." Thangachi grasps my feet in supplication, her braid sweeping the floor, and I feel the wetness of her tears on my feet, the salt in them searing the dry, cracked skin. There's pain behind my eyes, a kind of heat. "You will announce to the world that I delivered twins, a girl and a boy."

"Amma, what is this nightmare you are making happen? I need to think about all this. He is my son."

"Then I will think about whether I should kick you out of my house. Come with me. There is something I want to show you at the top of the stairs."

"Aiyo Amma, you won't kick me down the stairs, the way Athan kicked the dhobi?" Thangachi lifts her palm up.

"What happened to the dhobi is nothing compared to what I will do to you," I say as I lead her upstairs by her wrist.

THE INDRA QUARTET

I grab Thangachi to push her towards the kitchen. Her bangle snaps, cutting her left wrist and puncturing my right thumb. The blood oozes from our wounds to form two distinct rivulets.

"You don't have to wave harder or cry longer and louder than I," I say at the main gate. I nudge her elbow and jut out my chin, something I always do to show I am head of the household.

"Typical of you, making drama; clean the dirty blood off yourself and bring me a plaster."

"Dirty? We have the same blood," Thangachi mutters.

"Only when you were my little sister, a very long time ago."

"Once a sister, always…"

"You were anything but a sister when my husband was around nineteen years ago."

"Could I help it if KK wanted a wife who could give him a son?"

"Don't answer back." I thrust my hand at her face. "See what your pasar malam bangles did to me. Get out of my sight."

I think of the time when Thangachi had worn gold bangles. Our Amma had given us three sets each on our eighteenth birthdays. Thangachi didn't even deserve brass; plastic as cheap as she would have sufficed. "Now go back to your cooking."

Thangachi moves away, her head bent low. I watch as she dashes to the kitchen, pressing on the wound in her hand.

Raja's taxi arrives at 7.00am to take him to college in Singapore. I watch the driver load the boot with bags of new clothes and three books that I had bound in brown paper. Raja looks good, like my husband KK would have, in the blue shirt he is wearing. The previous night, I stitched the missing top button on it and slipped extra buttons into his suitcase, just in case.

I gather my son into my arms despite his protests that he can't make it at college. I reply that I swear he can and smother him with kisses. When Thangachi tried hugging him earlier, I had pushed the coir mat between them, causing her to stumble. By the time she pulled herself together, I had urged my boy out of the door. "My heir should travel in style," I tell Raja with hands outstretched. "Call Amma as soon as you reach college."

My daughter, Kumari, has less luggage and fewer hugs as she leaves with Raja. I decided to send her for orientation week to be my spy and give me a detailed report about Raja, as this is the first time he will be out of my sight for so long. Thangachi stands behind me outside the front gate. We both watch the taxi shrink to the size of a toy car before it vanishes round the corner.

"Light the camphor in the pooja room. I need to pray for my son's safe arrival and make a special prayer so that he won't have to struggle with his studies." The scent of incense sticks soothes me.

In my cushioned chair on the front veranda, I mull over life. I put on the plaster that Thangachi brings me, while a sparrow lands in a coconut tree and drops a twig. It is about to pick up a fallen seed when a screeching mynah, followed by a crow, flies down towards the seed and pushes the sparrow aside.

"So nice, waiting for me here," my neighbour, Mrs Chinniah, calls out.

"Er…come." I make a fist and hold my thumb down to suppress the flow of blood beneath the plaster.

"Keeping rice for the birds?"

"No, stopping a little blood…"

"Blood? Aiyo, what happened? Better wash and put a bandage."

"Small scratch only." I bind the tip of my cotton saree shawl around the cut and usher my friend in.

Mrs Chinniah collapses into the rattan chair. "What's your worry now?"

"That's what I need to talk to you about." I put on my silver-framed glasses to get a better look at the sleeve of Mrs Chinniah's choli blouse.

She begins to smoothen the frays. "What happened?" she asks.

"I sent Raja to study in Singapore and Kumari to be with him for orientation week because I can pay for only one to study there." I gather up the cardigan I am crocheting for my daughter.

"Isn't she the one who studies hard?" says Mrs Chinniah.

"Money for my boy's college education, I insist; property for both boy and girl." I rub the creases on my forehead, hoping to erase them.

"Break coconuts. Whether ten or one, Lord Ganesha will give answers. If not, sell your rubber estate and send Kumari to college also."

I hold up my thumb and forefinger, separate them two centimetres, and say: "Eh, it's only a small holding, under ten acres."

Mrs Chinniah opens her mouth wide. "I thought it was larger than that, the way you spend on Raja."

"Kumari is lost in her book world." I loop the pink wool around the crook of the hook. "It's Raja who drops at my feet asking what he can do for me. I reward him by sending him to college whether he appreciates it or not. He doesn't know what's good for him the way I do."

Thangachi emerges from within the house, hunched as she plods to the front yard. I get up and lean against the rails of the veranda, observing my sister splashing jasmine bushes with the water used for soaking rice.

I order Thangachi to serve Mrs Chinniah tea with milk, mixed with a teaspoon of sugar, and to bring along a glass of starfruit juice for me. Thangachi comes back with a glass of tea for Mrs Chinniah and a cup of juice for me. Gila woman. Does she do these things deliberately? She deserves a good beating for embarrassing me in front of my visitor.

Mrs Chinniah shifts in the chair. I signal her to lean forwards. "I have to show Thangachi that I'm fair to Raja."

"Why ah?" Mrs Chinniah pulls out a crumpled handkerchief from the folds of her waistline to dab her neck.

"That's a family worry. Don't let that pey there hear us." I tap my earlobes.

"You must share big problems with me as your best friend."

"Well, haven't I let you taste my best kolukattai, vadai and payasam? But some things have to stay that way." Bringing Raja's birth certificate to his principal's office is my own secret.

"Indra, it must be hard for you…" She takes a sip of the tea. "Hope not like the story we all heard from the gowerment quarters."

"About what?"

"Two sisters fighting over one baby," she says.

I wipe my cheeks with the back of my hand. "Not decent listening to rumours," I say.

"Your Raja brings you flowers. So, you love him more."

"I love my Kumari. But Raja brings me chocolates," I say with a smile.

"That will make your kneecaps melt."

"Yes, I get into a Thaipusam trance. If I carry a kavadi, it will be full of chocolates."

"Aiyo, that Raja rascal knows your soft spot. You seem to be bending over backwards to favour him."

I don't reply. Instead, I reflect on the moment when Raja and I parted. He was gritting his teeth as if in anger while I dabbed my eyes with my saree shawl.

A creak from Mrs Chinniah's chair pulls my thoughts back to the present. "You leaving?"

Mrs Chinniah points to the bougainvillea leaves settled on her Bata slippers, swept by the wind. "I don't want my umbrella to fly off again," she says. "That day, my Nylex saree stuck to my legs. It looked like I was dressed in blue pants. Cheee!"

On the first ring of the phone from the lounge table, I stand up with a start and pick it up. I am dying to hear my Raja's voice, but it is Kumari who says that they have arrived safely and that Raja is already busy making friends.

As I raise my hands together in gratitude, Thangachi stands on her toes to raise hers higher.

Raja is far away from me and now there's gossip about my secret. I must get rid of the curses looming over me. While I search through the kitchen cabinet for fresh turmeric roots, Thangachi offers to get them for me.

"No more bad luck from you," I say, as she hands a few stubs of the condiment to me. After selecting three limes from the kitchen table, I slit them across their top ends. I pull off the bath towel hanging from the clothesline and go upstairs to my bathroom. I rub the turmeric roots against a corner of the cement tub before mushing them into a paste. I press the limes one by one over my hairline, feeling the juice forming a puddle that trickles down my forehead and temples. I collect the turmeric paste, then scrub the soles of my feet. The biting scent fills my nostrils. Next, I gather the leftovers of my ritual and trace three circles clockwise, and then three anti-clockwise, around my figure, before dumping the mushy pulp into the sump pit. Finally, I splash a full dipper of water over myself. "Hit on me and sap my curses!" The citrusy fluid stings my eyes. It is a small price to pay.

At my dressing table, I dust powder from the hard tube of Cuticura. I recall feeding my children during their infancy. Many a time, when Kumari was absorbed in a book of fairy tales, I would take advantage of that to give Raja two mouthfuls in a row. I wipe away my tears, go up to the bed, pick up the pillows and fluff them up one by one. Near the date of Raja's departure, I had told Thangachi to prepare his choice of foods: murukku, archi murukku or chippi. I didn't want him to go hungry or miss any of my homemade goodies.

Raja's words when he was about to leave have since hounded me: "You want me to think of your or Thangachi's hard work when I eat all the fried stuff? What lah, Amma! Students in Singapore will think I am a village boy with food packed in rusty biscuit tins." Raja rolls his eyes.

"Raja, at least choose one."

When I reached out to caress Raja's cheek, he moved away. Thangachi witnessed it. Raja's Old Spice aftershave evoked miserable memories of KK. It was as if my KK were back to taunt me through Raja.

Thangachi intervened. "Raja…choose what you like; at least one for your Amma's sake…"

Raja took only the smallest bottle of chippi as a token. I felt the room spinning and held on to a high back chair. He frowned at me. "Amma, no drama, please." Thangachi smiled then.

When he saw my eyes moisten, he placed an arm around my shoulder. "Amma, let's not fight just as I am leaving. I might say something that hurts you."

His words pierced my heart deeper than Thangachi's broken bangles had when they slashed my thumb. The gold chain weighs heavy on my neck. Later, in the kitchen, I smack Thangachi for good measure for having dared to smile. I smack her a second time when I remember that evening, two weeks before Raja's departure, when I sat on the lounge sipping black tea from a cup engraved with KK's initials and overheard Thangachi in conversation with Kumari in the kitchen. She had told Kumari that her father would not touch his meals if I served him dinner; they were not to his taste. He would change from his sarong and singlet to a long-sleeved shirt and trousers to dine at his club. "Your papa never liked your Amma's recipes. So now you know why all cooking is left to me."

"Have you been cooking for my parents all these years?"

"Yes, nineteen years, since I lost my…"

"Who…? What?"

"My husband and my only child."

"Is that why Amma gave you a job and allowed you to stay at our home?"

"Partly."

"I'm so sorry to hear. I'm glad my Amma helped you. I should ask her to give you extra money for new clothes." Hearing this, I was furious.

"Tell me what else you want me to cook for you, I learnt many recipes from my late mother."

How dare she?

I hear Kumari leave the kitchen and I resume crocheting the nearly completed sweater I am making for her. She even asked if she could take it with her when she went away to study. I didn't tell her the truth then, that I had no plans for her further education.

Now I am glad that I paid for her trip to see Raja's college, at least.

Sleeping was difficult with both children away. The clock on the side table shows it's too early for breakfast, but I still get out of bed. I prepare a mug of Ovaltine and sit at the kitchen table to open a jar of Marie biscuits. I go to Raja's bedroom. I get a shock seeing Thangachi leaning against the wall in a corner. She is holding a book under the table lamp. It is that diary with "1952" engraved in silver on the cover. "What are you stealing?" I shout.

Thangachi drops the book and a few pictures fall out. "No, Amma. I am cleaning his room." She has picked up one of the photos to hide it behind her back.

I come up to her, shove her, and the photo slips and falls. It settles beneath the study table. I stoop to pick it up. It is a photo of KK holding baby Raja with Thangachi by his side. "One more secret you two kept from me?"

"No, Amma. Sorry, Amma."

I grab a pair of scissors from the puppy-shaped pencil holder on Raja's study table. As I begin to cut along Thangachi's profile she lurches forwards, and a part of KK's sleeve where she had leaned on his arm gets cut across. Thangachi goes down on her hands and knees; the tears stream across her face and drip onto the polished wood floor while she collects the cuttings I dump into a wastepaper basket.

"I suspect you were stupid enough to have shown this to Raja and told him that he is your son," I say, pulling her up by pinching her ear. "I should not spoil the only chance for our son's best education."

"I confess I tried but he totally refused to believe me," Thangachi says. She drops her head and covers her face. I am so relieved that Raja would not believe that he's a maid's son.

I open the diary. It is in Thangachi's handwriting, and tells of her one-year marriage to my husband, KK. I can't take it. I drop the book onto the bed before I wring the front of Thangachi's blouse until she confesses that, for years, she had hidden it safely in Raja's room. In between sobs and hitched breaths she tells me she had hoped to run away while carrying Raja as a baby. But with no money or a place to go to, she had no choice but to stay behind. This makes me shriek with laughter.

On Kumari's return home, I remind her to tell me everything that happened from the time Raja's taxi left our gate to the moment she said goodbye to him in Singapore. I tell Thangachi to bring Kumari our largest mug of Horlicks and a few slices of Sunshine bread with a double layer of kaya. Kumari gives me two boxes of chocolates from Raja. One imported, with almonds and pistachios, that he had surely bought for me; the other looks less fancy and is clearly a local product. It has to be for Thangachi. I take it to my room and lock it in a cupboard drawer and hide the key. I join Kumari on the veranda.

"Amma, let me try to recall the whole story for you."

"That's my kunju, what would I do without my extra set of eyes and ears."

"Amma, you saw Raja, sitting in the front. He pushed his seat far back, to show off his white pointed shoes to the driver. We saw miniature statues of Lord Ganesha, Buddha and Kwan Yin lining the dashboard and a rosary with a cross dangling on the front mirror. Raja asked, 'Annai, what is your religion?' The driver laughed. 'My father, Hindu. Mother, Christian. I got Buddhist and Taoist nephews from elder brothers. Somebody is our guardian angel, but donno who lah, thambi.' When Raja heard this, he turned around and asked me who his guardian angel was. Which one was Amma's? Which was mine? And Thangachi's especially, since Amma told us she has no family?"

"What a thoughtful son I have," I say.

"As the taxi passed Melaka, we watched the water buffalos pulling their ploughs. Raja said Amma shared her name, 'Indra', with the god of thunder and rain. He clasped his palms above his head and prayed for a sign of the divine Indra's courage and strength to pull him through his first year of college."

Just when I think that Kumari has covered the most important part of her account, she drags her chair closer to me and, in a lower tone, confides that during the first three days, Raja focused mostly on girls who smoked and dressed in jeans and T-shirts. He even invited them to restaurants and pubs. I am shocked, then wounded. Just like his father, I think, always with more than one girl swarming around him. Kumari reminds me that Raja's expenditure is pointless because the meals at the hostel have already been paid for. Then Kumari tells me that Raja took her to meet an astrologer in a shop along Serangoon Road in Little India.

"Oh, tell me everything about it," I say.

"The scents of incense and camphor led us directly to the astrologer's room. He was seated cross-legged on a large cushion with tassels. He looked at Raja, then at me. 'Born almost same time,' he said. Raja said, 'Yes, we are twins.' The astrologer shook his head and said, 'Sister, brother, not twins.'"

"What rubbish," I tell my daughter.

"Yes, Amma. He also said, 'Raja, going through bad period, this year fail, next year pass.' And you know what Raja said? 'No need to study this year since sure fail. Next year also, wasting time to study, since the fortune-teller says sure pass. Better enjoy myself here.'"

"More nonsense."

"I told Raja, better go home before Amma's money finishes," Kumari continues.

"You shouldn't have upset him."

"Raja wasn't angry, Amma. He asked if I were jealous he was having a good time, and pulled my ponytail." Kumari goes on to say she asked about the courses available in the following year and shows me the two brochures she had picked up. Through the kitchen door, I see Thangachi heating a pan of oil over the kerosene stove while mixing the ingredients for the batter and slitting three ripe bananas into halves to make Kumari's tea-time treat: pisang goreng.

"Are you trying to goreng your way into my girl's heart?" I call out. She crouches in silence.

I tell Thangachi to go to the mill once she clears the teacups. It is a regular chore I set for her. Thangachi asks me if Kumari can accompany her to the mill that evening. She needs help with carrying the cloth bags of chillies, coriander seeds, pepper and rice. I agree that Kumari can go on the condition that Thangachi doesn't take her through the government quarters.

Kumari places the bags in the basket on her bicycle. Thangachi shows her the blisters on her hands caused by the Clorox bleach and the steel-wire brush I had asked her to use for scrubbing the back drains. What cheek.

I spend my time in the living room trying to read my *Indian Movie News*. I can't get past the first page. Instead I sit, pulling the dark-blue threads jutting out around the peacock design I am stitching onto my throw pillow. I move to the window and look out for any sign of Kumari. After two hours, I spot her dragging her bicycle alongside Thangachi. I thank the gods that my daughter has returned. I must put a stop to Thangachi's cunning habit of tempting my Kumari with more outings. I order Thangachi to go into the kitchen through the back entrance before asking Kumari what happened.

Kumari says Thangachi complained that since they had heavy bags to carry up and down, my instruction to avoid the government quarters was stupid as it was the only shortcut to the mill and they would take it. They came across Mrs Kandiah, a former neighbour from when Amma and Papa had lived in the government quarters, choosing durians from a stall.

"Mrs Kandiah seemed to know a lot about our family in the early days. She asked Thangachi about our new home, which she heard was hidden away so no one could even peek into the garden. She asked how the children were getting on and said how lucky you are, Amma, to have two children to yourself, not like the two women who fought over one child whom some people still gossip about. She asked Thangachi if she knew the story. She helped me push my bicycle with the load across the street back home, Amma."

Kumari says that when she asked Thangachi why Mrs Kandiah's question had put her in such high spirits, Thangachi replied that I would know the answer.

I pull the long dark-blue thread between my teeth to bite it off. Oh Kadavulai, if Mrs Kandiah spills the beans to my pet Raja that Thangachi is his mother, that will destroy everything I have worked for. If Thangachi then challenges me to show who the mother named in Raja's birth certificate is, she will be signing my death certificate.

"Close the door," I say, tapping a ladle on the table while alone in the kitchen with Thangachi.

"Why, Amma? I haven't finished…"

"Don't answer back! Tell me what stories you used to poison my daughter's mind while dragging her everywhere," I shout.

"Nothing, Amma."

"You made her go with you to the mill through our old government quarters. If you grind chillies on my head, I'll squeeze them into your eyes."

I go up to the kerosene stove near where Thangachi is standing and tip the saucepan of leftover fish gravy from dinner onto her chest. Her nylon saree absorbs only part of the mixture, leaving a big oily patch behind. I notice a piece of tomato skin clinging to Thangachi's bare arm. "See what you made me do! Wasted fish curry!" I shout. "Next time, it will be something hot from the stove. How silly that I didn't throw you out on the road with only the clothes on you when they were babies."

Thangachi takes a wet towel that she normally uses to clean the table and dabs her blouse. She breathes heavily before gritting her teeth. As I turn and walk towards the main hall, I hear the brakes on Kumari's bicycle. I wait for her to come inside. When she does, she draws out a long blue envelope from her bag and spins it in her hand. She winks at me.

"Amma, a Singapore letter for you..."

I take it and tear its sides. I tremble as I unfold the letter.

My very dear Amma,

How are you without me to spoil you? I hope you liked the chocolates I sent. I shall bring you more with different fillings of caramel, almonds, jelly, strawberry cream in shapes of hearts, ovals, diamonds and triangles. All imported.

I spent the pocket money you gave me. Please send some more as everything here is expensive.

Amma, take care of yourself and remember to transfer the money to me ASAP.

Your loving son,
Raja

I fold the letter and tuck it under the left side of my choli.
My child. My own son, I shouldn't have sent him away.

I look up to where the tall pillars lining the walls of the bank end
in elaborately carved cornices. I start to feel dizzy. This is not the
first time I have had to come here to withdraw funds for Raja's
studies, yet my eyelids are twitching. I worry about the depleting
balance in my personal account.

"Amma..."

Kumari touches my arm. "Amma, how much this time?"

"Can you check, Kumari?"

She scans the account statement and then stops, pointing at
the final line. Her cry of surprise rises above the sounds of bills
being sifted and rubber stamps being pounded. A bank teller
stares at her; another peers at us from above his glasses before
resuming the work of jotting something down in an unusually
long book.

"Your balance is much lower than expected."

"Stop it, Kumari!" I hiss.

Two hours later, as I unlock the front door, I see Thangachi
running down the stairs. She picks up a pail with a rag cloth
wrapped around the handle.

I pour warm water from the kettle into a tumbler before
walking upstairs. "You better clear out all the cobwebs. Look at
the lizard droppings stuck to the walls for a year. If I see my
kitchen as dirty as you are, I will make sure you have only one
meal a day."

As I pass my daughter's bedroom, I notice something white and pointed under the door. I bend over and smell curry powder. While I am peeling the glue from the envelope, my fingers feel cooked rice. I suspect that the witch who sent this note to Kumari is Thangachi.

The letter asserts that Mrs Kandiah's story about two sisters fighting over a baby is true. It ends with the most obvious question: How could Kumari and Raja be twins when they have different birthdates and mothers? I sit on the single chair next to the bookshelf in front of Kumari's room and think furiously. I shout out loud, knowing it will send Thangachi's heart beating. I hear her as she rushes upstairs. She brings a broom and a dustpan.

"What is this?" I crush the note up and throw it at her.

Thangachi drops the dustpan. Before she can say anything, I walk up to her and tug at the black string on her neck. The broom falls from her grip.

"I told you before, stop your dirty tricks." I pull the string as hard as I can until it squeezes her neck and she is gasping for breath. Beads of sweat form under her eyes. She doesn't put up any resistance. I release her and she falls upon the floor.

"Amma, I don't want to live without my own son knowing who his real mother is."

Thangachi grabs the string around her own neck and starts to tighten it herself. As the string cuts into her blue–black neck and her eyes start to bulge, I suddenly have an image of a cot, as I helped our Amma rock baby Thangachi to sleep. I tear her grasp away from the string. Thangachi's body is damp and limp. Her neck is bathed in sweat and her eyes are wide with terror.

"You don't get to take your own life in my house," I say, while holding a tight fist against her chest. "You don't get to do anything unless I say so."

"Amma! What are you saying?" exclaims Thangachi as she rolls over onto her side.

I stand over her. "Get up, dry yourself and continue your housework."

She wraps her saree shawl over her neck to conceal the bruises.

Two weeks later, there is a knock on the front door. "Amma!" The door flies open and a weary Raja trudges in. I go up to him and hug him. He allows himself to be hugged. I ask him if it is a surprise holiday visit. He shakes his head. After a long silence, he says, "Amma, I was…forced to leave."

"Kadavulai. My God. Why? What wrong did you do?" I hug him again.

"It's not what wrong I did. It's what you did, Amma."

"Ai…aiyo, what are you saying, Raja? I have been here at home while you were in college."

"You knew very well that there was no way I could pass any exam in college."

"I want you to have the best chance in this life. You are Raja, you are my king."

"Maybe at school, but certainly not being pushed up to college."

"You are my only son."

Thangachi, who is dusting the rails on the bannister, walks slowly downstairs, her eyes on Raja.

"No, Amma, you didn't care that you forced me to make a fool of myself."

My mouth feels dry as I position myself between Raja and Thangachi. My body screens her out from his view. I don't want her any nearer than necessary.

"Raja, I have always taken good care of you." I try to hug him again.

"Only in the way you wanted to, Amma." Raja turns his back on me.

I lean forwards to try to curl Raja's hair around my fingers. "I kept my promise." I shiver for the first time since KK's death.

"Amma, what promise? To whom?"

Thangachi thrusts herself forward. She pulls her shoulders and her chin up higher than ever before since KK's death. She glares at me before switching to a triumphant smile towards Raja.

"Raja, Amma's promise to me to send you to university and not to favour Kumari when she adopted you from me." Thangachi touches Raja's chin and kisses the tips of her fingers.

For a moment, Raja does not move. He stands there, blinking at Thangachi. "What are you saying?"

"You are my own dear son." Thangachi's eyes brim with tears.

"Do not listen to her nonsense!" I screech.

"I refuse to believe that I am the son of a lowly maid," Raja says to Thangachi in a deadpan voice."

"Amma, so that is why you always favoured Raja over me?" Kumari's voice rises.

"Kumari, you are also my own child, like Raja." Thangachi smiles.

"Amma, I thought Thangachi was fantasising when she told me her stories after meeting Mrs Kandiah with me."

"No, my kunju. Not true at all, I swear." I hug Raja, who no longer even tries to shrug me off. He looks at me in shock. I turn to hug my Kumari, going back and forth between my children. Kumari peels my fingers off her shoulder. "Amma, why did you treat even my stepbrother better than me?"

"I had sworn to Thangachi that I wouldn't favour you over him, but I overdid it. It was easy to do that—we naturally favour sons."

Thangachi brays, "Both of you were adopted from me." Suddenly, Raja punches a fist against his palm.

"Thangachi, what are you saying?" Kumari says.

"Kumari, you remember the lady from the government quarters talking about two women arguing over a baby?" Thangachi says.

"Yes," Kumari says.

"Those two sisters were Amma and I fighting over both of you."

"Amma, which one of you is trying to fool us?" Raja kicks the flowerpot beside the front door. "Thangachi, why didn't you shout out your claim earlier instead of just hinting? All the money could be ours."

The flowerpot skids across the floor, scattering petals and dried earth. I look down at the broken pot as it comes to rest at my feet.

"Raja, if I had done that, Amma wouldn't have pampered you all these years," Thangachi says.

"There is very little money left in the family for any more pampering," I confess.

Thangachi brushes past me. She makes no attempt to clean up the earth and petals, but waves her wrist at me so that I can see the healed scar where the broken bangle had cut her. A smile hovers on her lips.

"Amma, do you dare to repeat your words in front of Mrs Kandiah, who knows the true story?"

I don't know what will now become of my life, of my happiness, of my family.

If Mrs Kandiah confirms her story, will Thangachi then dare to challenge me to show the mother's name in Raja's birth certificate? I may have to treat her much better from now on.

There is a knock at the door.

"It's Mrs Kandiah from the government quarters," says the voice through the door.

FREE AND FREED

"How arr you, I hope." Mrs Kandiah peered over her glasses at her confidante, Mrs Chelliah, who had rushed through the open front gates of her home. Mrs Kandiah's glasses were perched so precariously on the tip of her long nose that they might topple if she were to sneeze.

"Simplee, Mrs Kandiah."

"Leave out your usual simple talk. You say I am your senior-most friend. So tell, tell, what are really happening. We moral police must know about every moral crime committed in our own community. When one of our baby monkeys does anything wrong, it brings shame to every one of our people, especially we all parents."

Mrs Kandiah tightened her large hair bun. She had been tending her garden, whether it needed it or not. The lush bougainvilleas, hibiscus, jasmines and orchids were such a delicate contrast to the correct Hindu-temple-peacock-blue façade of her house, the colour of the 1950s. Such solace her garden gave her, such a grand view of her neighbours' comings, goings, doings and un-doings.

"Nothing serious. Small matter only, Mrs Kandiah."

"For you everything is small. Just because you are small-built, and you have a tiny kondai behind your head, you don't have to be small-minded also. Small secrets become big scandals. Have you heard of small pregnancies, oh mother of more than two grown-up children? Stop chewing your betel leaf like a lazy baby buffalo and start spitting straight."

On seeing Mrs Chelliah arrange her fingers in a V shape on her lips, Mrs Kandiah said, "Your story I mean, not your betel-red mouthful of saliva. I know you can hit a bull's-eye with your betel-leaf-saliva. Now tell telegram style and save money and time."

Mrs Chelliah grabbed Mrs Kandiah's right forearm to pull her towards herself.

"Muthiah's daughter out all alone at night with—of all things—a boy! Poor Muthiah, all daughters with dowries to drown for and no sons to collect back in return. What a wretched life. Finance clerk Retnam says Muthiah's dowry account is a one-way street." She choked on the betel-nut juice as she caught her breath. "All payments and no income. He only got a government pension."

"So graduate bridegroom must be too expensive for him." Mrs Kandiah's large eyes turned upwards as she screwed up her nose. "Don't dare dream of doctor. Even an engineer or lawyer son-in-law cannot reach. He is expected to be weak and silent. Not like the heroes in the English films I saw in the Rex Cinema."

"You remember what happened to Muthiah's eldest daughter? On the wedding day, guests all seated and priest ready to start ceremony with prayers for Lord Ganesha to remove all obstacles. Before priest could appeal to Lord Ganesha, bridegroom refused to enter wedding hall before ceremony unless full cheque put on tray before him…" Mrs Chelliah's voice modulated to a conspiratorial whisper. Mrs Kandiah stuck her face close to Mrs Chelliah's.

Mrs Chelliah leaned forward, her lips almost touching the whorl of Mrs Kandiah's ear, even though it was just the two of them in the garden. "Muthiah complained that boys are given more freedom. Some abuse it by choosing girlfriends and, worse still, brides from outside our community. So, the number of eligible boys available for our well-brought-up and protected girls at home is even lower." She noted Mrs Kandiah nodding away with satisfaction. "Parents of boys, especially doctor boys, are demanding huge sums, like extortion money, in the presence of priest. This is like brownmail. Is this fair, I ask you, Mrs Kandiah?"

"Mrs Chelliah, when I asked you to tell all, I din' mean you can include a lecture on the dowry system. I definitely don't need it. Just because you have two daughters to my one, it doesn't make you a double expert on daughters. Concentrate on your main news. When a boy and girl go out alone at night without a chaper-one or a chaper-two, even broad-minded people will think something. What about us? We won't stop thinking."

"Because we all such thoughtful people." Mrs Chelliah pressed her fingers on her forehead.

"Children can watch adult films till they're blue–black but matchmaking must be under parents' direction, not simplee just guidance. Two families' honour disgraced already. Mere murders any roadside detective can solve. Who is this jackal, ripping apart our community's sacred customs?" Mrs Kandiah tugged at the dried leaves wound around the fence.

"That all we must find out."

"Must be an evil orphan, badly brought up by a dog worse than all other dogs."

"Will he bite us?"

"Not if we ambush him first. He'll either beg us to arrange a Sten-gun marriage or commit suicide. Where does he carry out his deadly deeds?" Mrs Kandiah shook the garden scissors in the air before she slipped it back into its plastic cover.

"Gossipers say he loafs around the Lido Cinema on Friday evenings when all decent people are at our temple."

"We'll go there this Friday." Mrs Kandiah attacked the weeds ferociously with her changkul before placing the marigold seedlings in a row. "In front of everyone, I'll clear my throat and spit. Then I'll take off my slipper and shake it in his face. I better hold it really close to that dirty fellow."

"Why?"

"So I make sure he can see every grain of dirty sand on the back of this slipper. He will know how many miles the wearer of these slippers has walked and how much more about life she knows than this puppy. No, no, I won't call him puppy, it makes that devil sound cute."

"Then what name to give him?" Mrs Chelliah giggled.

"I'll call him that 'dirty small dog'. If he comes near my house, I will let loose my outstation dog on him."

"You mean your Alsatian dog?"

"No need to repeat after me, I am your elder, not your school-teacher. After that terrible insult, he won't have any face left to show in Kuala Lumpur, Singapore or any other Pore. He'll be forced to be a hermit or to commit 'hari kira' or whatever kira the Japanese call it when they do it, or simple suicide when anybody else does it."

Mrs Kandiah watered the plants stem by stem. She tapped her slipper over the grassy patch, rinsed her feet and hung the garden hose over the fence; water was still dripping.

Mrs Chelliah tightened the tap while she told her friend to make sure it was her slipper she would be holding in front of his shameful face and not her own purse. He might snatch it, the way he grabbed poor Muthiah's daughter from her innocent parents and family.

"Mrs Chelliah, I am old enough to tell the difference between a purse and a slipper. I know exactly how to punish rascals with

my mouth. I just burn their thick skins with my chilli padi words."
Mrs Kandiah snapped red and green chillies from her vegetable
plot. She remarked that her slippers came out only for dealing
with very serious crimes.

"Like what?"

"Those worse than murder. I don't break people's kneecaps. I
leave that to our menfolk who don't have the power of a sharp and
spicy tongue. This is the best weapon we women know. When I
want, I can make it more deadly than any kneecap breaker, as our
little Lido lover will find out tomorrow. My hot tongue will slice
him until that rascal's face has as much blood as your mouth has
red saliva."

Mrs Chelliah stroked Mrs Kandiah's shoulder, saying that she
was their whole community's heroine. "Mrs Kandiah, some say
in Ammrika and England all the world louvoes a louvoer."

"Ammrika, kathrika. Maybe in God-forsaken places, but not
in our part of the world. Here, all the world and their parents
love an arranger, a marriage broker or the parents of an eligible
boy, and not a lowly lover who has no respect for his parents or
other people's parents."

Mrs Kandiah gave, or not so much gave as shook at, Mrs
Chelliah a bunch of hibiscus and a few chilli padis.

That night, Mrs Kandiah slept restlessly, wrestling with nightmares about surprises and shocks, and talked in her sleep. "I
never miss Friday evening prayers, but I'm doing Lord Ganesha's
work in the cinema this Friday."

She woke even earlier than usual, well before the sun dared
rise on her. She recalled her childhood when everything had
been arranged for her sisters by her parents, with no place for

anything startling. It was her duty now to be equally maternal towards the new generation in the Jaffna Tamil community of Malaya. She did not want to witness yet another stain on their community. She could not forget when her cousin, whom she was close to, had been forced to elope. "If only I had been guarding her house gate," she whispered to Mrs Chelliah.

At 5.45pm, Mrs Kandiah strode into the Lido Cinema with Mrs Chelliah skipping to keep up. At the foyer, the two ladies inhaled the competing fragrances of the white-and-yellow strands of jasmine around the hair buns of saree-clad ladies and the chemical perfumes of the non-saree-clad women. Several electrical fans were beating away at maximum speed. Mrs Chelliah used her saree shawl to wipe the sweat dripping down her neck, while Mrs Kandiah let her handheld fan work for her. Mrs Chelliah looked out for Muthiah's daughter among the girls selecting kachang putih, kuachi, assam buah and sliced nutmeg at stalls lined below the curved stairway. Mrs Kandiah looked past patrons ogling their favourite film stars twitching their moustaches in sword-fighting duels and heroines fluttering their eyelashes on blown-up photographs, to search for Ms Muthiah.

"Mrs Chelliah, imagine this rogue once the lights are switched off, corrupting her with a K and C."

"Kueh kochi and curry pup?"

"Aiyo, a kiss and a cuddle. Even our un-shy Tamil film stars don't kiss on the screen. This dirty devil may act in his own underworld sideshow throughout the film."

"There's Muthiah's daughter, holding her books, trying to look as if she is on her way to the library."

Mrs Kandiah followed Mrs Chelliah's pointed finger as Muthiah's daughter headed for the ticket counter behind a metal grille. Mrs Chelliah's gaze landed on a sedate young man dressed immaculately, in a white shirt and trousers, in striking contrast to the multicoloured, gaudy glitter of reds, greens, maroons, pinks and violets of most of the patrons.

"Oh, look at who is waiting there. Our culprit leaning on the counter. Peria big shot." Mrs Chelliah nudged Mrs Kandiah.

"Ay you thambi," Mrs Kandiah accosted him, walking right up with her saree swishing, as she lowered the shawl wrapped around her shoulder to spread over her forearm. "You are surely not religious since you are at the cinema instead of the temple on a Friday evening. Like my favourite deity, Lord Ganesha, I too believe that everyone should be given a second chance to repent before they are punished. But you better say your prayers. You will be needing them fully for what I have to say to you. I am Mrs Kandiah, also known as Kaiser Kandiah, and this is Mrs Chelliah, better known as Chatterbox Chelliah. She talks a lot; it is all harmless and I keep a tight check on her. Now you confess your full name, your nickname, your father's name and his nickname."

"I'm Rajeswaran, son of Railway Rajadurai."

"Oh, you are the son of our powerful station master who runs our sothi express in the morning and murungakkai mail in the afternoon. Then, why are you behaving like a railway porter's shameless puppy?" Mrs Kandiah swiped down her index fingers over her cheeks.

"We mean dirty little dog?" Mrs Chelliah whispered from behind Mrs Kandiah.

"Shh…" Mrs Kandiah pushed aside Mrs Chelliah's shoulder. "Do you have any kind of job? Are you a loafer or a full-time unpaid attendant at this cinema?"

"I'm a doctor."

Mrs Kandiah oscillated the paper fan over her face. She was perspiring profusely despite the relatively less hot tropical sun in the late afternoon. "Doctor? Doctor…?" Mrs Kandiah cupped her mouth.

"Maybe you are one of those Pee-hDs who can't even spell aspreen or prescribe panadoll but call themselves doctor?" Mrs Chelliah said.

"Shameless fellows, misleading the poor public but not both of us aunties here." Mrs Kandiah directed a pointed finger at Mrs Chelliah and herself, although her finger wasn't held quite as straight as it had been before.

"No, I'm not one of those." Dr Rajeswaran shook his head.

"You mean to say that you are a Doctor? D-O-C-T-O-R doctor?" She asked if he meant to say that he is absolutely certain and very sure he is none other than a medical doctor? "You mean to tell us that you are one of those rare gifts from Lord Ganesha who, with one injection, ten or twelve tablets and two or three multicoloured mixtures, can cure any disease known to man and turn a pale and panting patient into a dancing deity like our Lord Shiva?" Mrs Kandiah's fingers remained over her chest.

"Do you have bad handwriting? My son also had such bad foul scratching, like a chicken after a worm," Mrs Chelliah interjected. She continued that she had been so sure he was going to be a doctor, but he turned out to be a pharmacist. "Now he has to read every doctor's bad scribble. Poor fellow."

"Stop interrupting me with small talk, Mrs Chelliah. Excuse me, Doctor, what a lovely surprise to meet a real doctor, not in a crowded clinic or in an overcrowded and unhealthy hospital but of all the unholy, unlikely, un-everything places, at the cinema." Mrs Kandiah lifted the shawl of her saree to cover her head.

Mrs Kandiah said that all the other characters there were wearing colourful costumes, shiny jewellery and all kinds of wigs. Doctors could afford anything but they just wore a simple white coat and a stethoscope for a necklace and they could cure the whole world. What wonderful and wise wizards they all were.

"By the way, a minor matter. How will Muthiah pay for his daughter's dowry?" Mrs Chelliah asked.

"I won't take a cent. I want to marry his daughter, not his money."

"Even without your miracle medicine, you can heal with your wise words." Mrs Kandiah's saree and her hair bun swayed in rhythm to the momentum of her speech. She said she agreed with him. Why should suffering, tortured parents get into debt and give away their life savings as dowries to all kinds of rowdies?

"Muthiah and his daughter are really smart," Mrs Chelliah said.

Mrs Kandiah could not imagine her getting a real medical doctor, not one of those many accountants, arts graduates, engineers, government officers, lawyers or those "Pee-hD fellows", completely and totally free of all forms of dowry.

"This only happens in the most fantastic of fantasy Tamil films. Never in real life." Both of Mrs Kandiah's palms turned upwards towards her forehead as if in supplication. She tipped back her head to look at the doctor. She said that the doctor's love marriage would set free all the unlucky parents with daughters. Free from the dowry sentence they had been condemned to from the very day their poor daughters were born without a brother to receive a marriage dowry in exchange. That he was not only a doctor but also a saint.

"What a great combination," sighed Mrs Chelliah.

"You will be a king not only in this world but also in the next. Who can beat that? You are greater than Abraham Lincoln or even Mahatma Gandhi. You set free the oppressed." Mrs Kandiah leant towards Dr Rajeswaran's ear. She had a secret to share with him.

"By the way, such long queues at your hospital. We people don't believe in those Western formalities about appointments, calling secretaries and whatnot-aries. We are simple straightforward saree-wearing aunties with our hair in kondai buns. Our only make-up is talcum powder."

"We just wear slippers, none of those high-heeled shoes and high expenses." Mrs Chelliah pointed to the young ladies on stilettos.

"You're free now, easier to consult you freely and for free here while we are still alive and talking. People have died while waiting for their medical appointments. I have this high blood pressure for a highly long time. Sweet, little Mrs Chelliah's diabetes is getting deadly… What is your advice, honourable DOCTOR Rajeswaran?"

As Mrs Kandiah swung her head sharply once more towards Dr Rajeswaran to curry favour, her tightly tied hair bun broke free. Her hair sprayed itself with her loosened greying locks all over her shoulders. She slumped, dragging the saree shawl just over her heels on flat slippers.

Mrs Kandiah did receive free advice. Dr Rajeswaran even invited her to come into his clinic for further consultations. Dr Rajeswaran's intended bride appeared to relax as Dr Rajeswaran talked; there was no longer any need to pretend she was en route to the library.

Mrs Chelliah's eyes seemed to have grown bigger while both her hands tried to cover her mouth in multiple directions. She had an acute attack of uncontrollable chuckles all the way home from the cinema.

RANI TAXIS AWAY

I'm starting a new life today.

I pull my old school uniform out of the cupboard and toss it into the wastepaper basket in the corner. From my window, I see Amma snipping off the dried bougainvillea flowers. They compete for attention with her heliconias, hibiscus, honeysuckles, jasmines and orchids. Amma and I argue because it's not just the flowers she likes well manicured; she says my taste in gardening, and in many other things, is too wild. My reflection in the window pane allows me to assess myself in my new outfit—a temple-blue saree which Amma gave me—for my first day as a temporary teacher at my alma mater, St Mary's. I see a young woman. There's a mole above her left eyebrow. Amma warns me that the mole's positioning predicts a major conflict between my family and me in my horoscope. Unlike Amma, I don't bother about it.

Amma is glad of the ample garden. She tells me the plants will distract her from her worries about my future. She's proud of this expansive new house on stilts on a corner lot on Scott Road in Kuala Lumpur. As she keeps reminding me, we wouldn't have it all without Papa's civil-service promotion following Merdeka last year. We have come up in the world, and I must always be mindful of that.

"Poitu varen." I leave and come back. Downstairs, Amma holds my cheeks in her palms, kisses my forehead and blesses me. "Lord Ganesha will remove all obstacles in your path to your new career. Aren't you glad that your Papa and I have arranged everything so that you don't have to sit alone, behind some young ruffian?"

A middle-aged private taxi driver gets out of his old Morris Oxford to open the door. "Good morning, Amma. I, Chandran."

To call someone "Amma", or "mother", is a mark of great respect. Yet here is this older man calling me "Amma". What if I say, "I am too young to be your Amma"? He may feel that I am making fun of him. I don't want to hurt his feelings even if my Amma says he's only a taxi driver. What's wrong with that? I don't agree with her about higher and lower classes or castes.

This is the first time in my life that I have been alone in a taxi. Papa or my younger brother always sits at the front, while Amma and I never sit anywhere except at the back, as we are expected to do. I stroke the reddish-brown upholstery. The smell of the old leather competes with the fresh jasmine garland around the tiny gold statue of Lord Ganesha on the dashboard. I inhale both scents. The sight of my Lord reassures me. I won't fear any obstacles. We overtake a bus crammed with men and boys on my familiar trip to school. My brother Tharma is probably on it.

When I report to the school office, the clerk, Azizah, tells me that after Merdeka, the British expatriate teachers—including my favourite English teacher, Ms Jones, and my Geography teacher, Mrs Tresise—went home to England. Only my headmistress, Ms Carpenter, stayed behind.

As I walk along the veranda, I admire the grand houses on Treacher Road. I turn to look back and I'm delighted to see Ms Carpenter's familiar pale face as she leads a cluster of new Malayan teachers of various skin colours around the building.

I approach the teachers' staff room. The whole school seems smaller, the ceilings lower than in my earliest memories of it, but the staff room remains just as large as before. As a student, I had to knock and ask for permission to return a poetry book to Ms Jones. I could peek in, but entering was a perk. Now, being a temporary teacher, I can open the old teak door and stride in. However, I still knock out of habit.

The familiar voice of my Mathematics teacher says, "Come in."

"Good morning, Ms Foo."

"Rani, you don't have to call me Ms Foo anymore. You are now my colleague and equal. Call me Siew Mun."

"Yes, Ms Foo Siew Mun."

"No, just Siew Mun."

As a student, I had nicknamed her Yong Tau Foo—stuffed soya bean curd—so it is a big change for me to call her "Siew Mun". Now that I am a teacher, I have to give up my mischievous schoolgirl habit of giving irreverent nicknames to all my teachers. The tea lady, Caroline, comes around for orders for Boh tea or local coffee. I ask for hot Milo.

Mrs Lee frowns. "Aiyoh! This is so childish, like a Primary-1-level girl asking for a sweet chocolate drink."

But I persist. Then, as Azizah gives me my timetable so I can start teaching from tomorrow, I swallow hard.

The next morning, Amma teases me, "Rani, this is the first time I have knocked on your bedroom door to find you already up without my coming back to knock a few more times. It's only your second day as a teacher. You must love your new job."

I smile in response. If I say anything in any direction, she may start organising my job for me. Breakfast is whatever Tharma orders. Amma asks only him.

Although I'm now a school ma'am, it's hard for me to change my habits. When the bell rings for my first class on my second day in school, I enter from the door at the back instead of the main entrance. I hesitate to sit at the teacher's desk to take the roll call. I must remember to bring my vase and some flowers to place on my desk. The sight of my much-loved yellow dancing-lady orchids from Amma's garden will make me relax. I tremble as I introduce myself to the forty pairs of eyes watching me. Perhaps these 13-year-olds are waiting to make fun of me the way I used to tease new teachers with my classmates. I hear some giggling, but pretend I don't. I'm not ready to deal with that yet. I have not been for my teacher training course yet, so for their Geography class I use lessons from my student days, using the same famous Commonwealth-set textbook by Sir Dudley Stamp and Dr GED Lewis. Dr Lewis is Tharma's headmaster at the Victoria Institution. I am relieved that the girls who had been restless at first are actually listening to me.

When I reach home, Amma is excited. "How was it, Rani? Did you enjoy work today?"

"My hands were trembling and I started my class with a stammer."

She hugs me and says, "That shows how much you care about your work. Don't worry. All that nervous feeling will go away soon."

She is right; it soon does.

Before I know it, a month has passed.

One day, after school in the taxi, I notice Chandran is grinning all the way, "You look extra happy today, Chandran."

"Today my payday, Amma. I going to buy kueh for my mother and sister."

"This is my payday, too. Where are you going to buy cakes, Chandran?"

"Kampam Bahru, Amma."

"Okay, take me there, please; I want to buy some for my family too. Do you always buy kueh?"

"No, Amma, I buy one month one time only. I saving money to buy secondhand taxi."

"Why not a new one?"

"I want to make taxi business. After Merdeka, people getting promotion, new, new jobs. So many buying new cars, so second-hand cheaper now. Best time to buy." Chandran raises his thumb as if he were little Jack Horner.

He is much smarter and more ambitious than Amma thinks he is. I catch him stealing glances at me in the rear-view mirror; my face feels warm. I am impressed and curious. Almost all my family and relatives are government servants. I don't personally know anyone who has new business dreams instead of old government ones.

"My family don't know anything about business. Can I learn from you?"

I like Chandran's shy smile in the rear-view mirror. He slows down near the kueh stall. I recall what Azizah had said about the old-world charm of Kampam Bahru and it is indeed just like a rural village in the middle of the town. When he pulls up his umbrella-handled handbrake, I get out. He trails behind. Amma's favourite, kueh lapis, with its layers of light pink and pastel purple, catches my eye first. Next, Papa's choice of the dark-brown crust and beige body of kueh bengkang, made from tapioca and brown sugar. Then my brother's favourite, the gluti-nous-rice pulut inti with grated coconut and gula Melaka brown sugar wrapped in a banana leaf. Then, pulut with a thick layer of golden-brown kaya jam, which my cousins like.

I ask Chandran what kueh he is buying and find myself smiling at him. He blushes. Most of the time, what I see of him is the back of his head and a rolled handkerchief covering the back of his collar. Today, looking at him full in the face, I notice the way his moustache moves when he smiles or talks.

Finally, I turn to my favourite kueh talam, the top half white with coconut milk and the bottom half a dark green. The aroma of the pandan leaves hits my nose as I take deep, joyous breaths. An older lady standing next to me tells me that the kueh seller, Haji Noh, with his white cap and shirt and his green sarong, is particularly proud of his kueh talam. He demonstrates this pride not only by his regular attire's similar colour scheme but also by painting the roof of his house santan white and the outer walls daun-pandan green. My eyes are engrossed in my kueh frenzy. A familiar voice intrudes to pull me back to earth.

"Hello Rani, what are you doing here?" It is Mrs SV (Strong Views) Kandiah. She is known as the local busybody or agony aunt. I imagine her high beak sniffing over me instead of the sweet daun pandan. She will have more stories to tell about my floral perfume.

"Er…I'm buying kueh, Mrs Kandiah," I stammer.

"Are you here alone?"

"No, er, Chandran is here with me."

"Chandran? Who's he?"

"My taxi driver."

Mrs Kandiah gives Chandran such a glare that he remains looking down, silent.

"Remember the old Malay proverb, pagar makan padi? This pagar is trying to eat the rice padi it should be protecting. You innocent little girl. Come, I will rescue you immediately from this cunning kidnapper and take you home safely in our car before anything terrible happens to you."

Embarrassment sweeps over my face; my throat feels tight with anger but I can't lash out at an elder.

"No, Mrs Kandiah."

"Listen, if a young girl like you makes one mistake, she will have to pay for it the rest of her life. I can help you choose the kueh. Since when did taxi drivers specialise in choosing cakes?"

"No, Mrs Kandiah, I chose the kueh on my own. It's at home that I don't get to choose anything."

"So who is this lowly taxi-driver fellow who dares to take you anywhere else but from home to school and back?"

"No, Aunty. It's not like that at all," I protest, returning to my more usual mild-spoken manner when addressing my community elders.

Mrs Kandiah raises her notorious eyebrows. "Does your mother know about this?"

"No, she doesn't but you see, I wanted to surprise her with some kueh."

Mrs Kandiah looks disbelieving. She wags her forefinger at me. "Rani, I'm going to tell your mother about this."

"No, no, Mrs Kandiah, I'm the one who asked him to bring me here." I'm about to cry. I'm afraid she's going to create a commotion. People are already beginning to stare at both of us and especially at me.

"I'm going to your house now. Rani, you better come along." Her voice brooks no argument, its stentorian tone almost casting a spell. To avoid creating a scene, maybe I should go with her. Mrs Kandiah says if I don't get into her car, she'll report Chandran. There's nothing for it; I gesture to Chandran to go back on his own and climb into the back seat of Mrs Kandiah's car. Mr NV Kandiah (No Views, because he always goes his wife's way) is at the wheel. He greets me as if he hadn't just witnessed his wife bossing me around. He tries to be like royalty—above the fray.

What an irony. It is not Chandran but this busybody, Mrs Kandiah, who is kidnapping me.

I turn back and see Chandran stumbling into his taxi, people pointing at him. Kadavulai! What is going to happen now? Is Mrs Kandiah going to tell my mother that she saw me in a strange place and, worst of all, with a strange man? Worse, she may even broadcast this information to our whole community and it may reach my school.

Mr Kandiah stops his car at our front gate. Mrs Kandiah gets out and he drives off to park the car. He looks relieved not to have to be involved in his wife's melodrama.

"Mrs Chinniah, you won't believe what I saw at the kueh stall," Mrs Kandiah calls out to my mother.

"What happened?" Amma looks first at Mrs Kandiah, then at me, and back again at Mrs Kandiah kicking her slippers off.

Mrs Kandiah sinks into one of the government-issue rattan armchairs in our lounge.

"I saw your Rani with a strange man in Kampam Bahru."

"Is this true, Rani?" Amma glares at me.

"Amma, I just asked Chandran to take me to buy kueh for the family."

"I'm not sure about this Chandran felloo," Mrs Kandiah tells Amma. "I've just saved your daughter's honour from that man. He says he's her taxi driver but he is taking her to out-of-the-way places."

"No, Mrs Kandiah. I know you have a keen sense of rumour but it's true; Chandran is the taxi driver we arranged to take her to school and back. Her Papa chose him."

Mrs Kandiah raises her eyebrows again.

"It's much safer than letting her travel alone in public buses. Our young men won't even give up their seats for our girls. Instead, they will be up to monkey tricks."

"Monkey tricks, donkey tricks. What do you think your Crocodile Chandran is up to? Has he been charming you also with his kueh tricks and treats? I am going to call our Road Transport Thillainathan to cancel this kueh-luring crocodile's taxi licence. Once we have chopped off his wheels, he will be crawling on his knees in his squatter hut. We will break his rice bowl. Then as the French queen Marionette Anthony or something said, let him eat kueh since you won't be feeding him his daily bread. That's what our convent nuns taught us."

"I don't know any French queens, Mrs Kandiah, but Chandran was well recommended to us."

"Which fool recommended him?"

"Your Dr Muthurajah."

Mrs Kandiah's face turns red. She takes leave briskly, her teacup still filled to the brim as she walks away to her car.

Amma turns to me. "You should know better than to do this, Rani. Next time, be careful. People will gossip all sorts of things."

"What do you mean, Amma?"

"We hired Chandran to take you only to school and back. Don't wander about with him. He might turn the mole over your eyebrow into a bad omen for our whole family. Young and unmarried girls don't roam about on their own. I have to talk to your father and your brother about this."

"Tharma? He is only fifteen."

"Yes, but he is a male in our family. Amma and you must ask what your Appa and thambi think first, before we both say what we think."

"Amma, that was generations ago."

"Your Papa and Tharma will know best. They are men of the world. They are our world. We live in our little convents. Our safety comes first. Because we listen to them, they shelter us."

"Amma, I am now a teacher. A guru. Tharma is just a pupil. He cannot have any say at all in what I do. I'll choose my own husband and he can select his own wife later." I stand up and look Amma in the eye the way I do with my students. I focus on my breathing and feel my shoulders squaring. "Amma, there is a new Rani at home now." Amma closes the front door and shuts her eyes as if to stifle the big subject I had just opened. She changes topic. "We should find a husband for you soon."

"No hurry burry, Amma, I am just starting to experience my own independence."

"You know how sharp Mrs Kandiah's tongue is. If you try to be too independent, she will put not only you but also our whole family in our place. After your Papa's promotion, we have even more face to lose.

"Rani, maybe you don't know that Mrs Kandiah has not had a happy marriage and it is only that she doesn't want other girls to make the mistake of a marriage they might later regret. It is why she insists so much on traditional behaviour and parents choosing husbands for their daughters and wives for their sons, because parents are sure to know better."

"Even if they regret their own marriage? But I didn't know that about Mrs Kandiah, Amma. Thank you for telling me."

"I don't like to talk about others. I don't know whether to protect you or to envy you and wish you well."

"I don't want to stay a prisoner in a convent forever, however secure that may be, Amma. I'm not scared of Mrs Kandiah. Doesn't Mrs Chong call her a busybody? Who is she to bully us? Who is she to control everyone in our community? Why are we afraid of her? Who does she think she is that she gets to lecture me about my own life?"

"Don't listen to Mrs Chong; she doesn't fully understand. Mrs Kandiah is very caring about our Jaffna Tamil community, Rani." Amma sighs. "She upholds the morals in our community. Our community's standing after Merdeka is in no small part due to her."

I feel torn. I understand that for Amma and many in the community there are deep roots, whereas I feel like a bird, a bird that wants to fly. Besides, what proof is there that Mrs Kandiah is such a great benefactress? I fold my fingers into my palms to stop their trembling. Amma looks out of our window at our driveway.

I suddenly can't bear to be in the sitting room with Amma. I understand everything she is saying, but this is not a good day for lukewarm tea and kolukattai.

The next morning, I find myself getting up even earlier. I press a bit more face powder to cover my mole. Amma would be glad not to see it.

In the taxi with Chandran, I say, "I'm sorry I was dragged away yesterday." He looks embarrassed, his eyes not quite meeting mine as his fingers grip the steering wheel harder than usual. At a junction, I see through my window a couple huddled on the bench at a bus stop sharing and reading one newspaper. Chandran sees them, too.

"So romantic," I catch myself saying.

"Saving money also," he replies.

We both giggle. The tension breaks.

All day at school, I keep tossing in my mind Amma's and Mrs Kandiah's words, and next I think of Chandran's moustache and our shared giggle. What will my senior teachers say in our staff room if they hear Mrs SV Kandiah's version of my innocent kueh-buying trip? I think the junior teachers will be on my side. Still, I hope they don't hear anything about this until Chandran has bought his second taxi. Then I can say that he is a businessman who is so careful about saving, not, as Mrs Kandiah and even mild Amma say, "just a taxi driver".

Ms Foo interrupts my thoughts. "Rani, I overheard some of our girls saying that they enjoyed your Geography lesson. I am proud of you as my ex-student. Maybe someday you can join me as a permanent teacher."

I am thrilled.

After school, I get back into our taxi. What goes on in here is my first chance to be an adult, an independent adult. School, where the girls look up to me to answer all their questions, is my other chance. In my taxi, I even get a middle-aged man who looks up to me. This has never happened to me before. It feels strange, but I love it.

"Let's go to a different stall today. Do you know any just outside KL?"

"Yes, Amma. Got good, good one in Kajang. Must ask your mother first?"

"No need to ask her anymore, Chandran."

"Are you very sure, Amma?"

"Yes, I want to taste the satay with its famous gravy there. A new place for a new Rani."

Chandran beams. The speed at which he is driving now seems to be different than usual.

I begin to feel a bit dizzy sitting in the back seat, and ask Chandran if I might sit up front with him.

ABOUT
THE AUTHOR

M. Shanmughalingam's short stories and poems have appeared in more than thirty anthologies and broadcasts by Buku Fixi, BFM 89.9, the British Council, Dewan Bahasa, EPB, Evans Brothers, Fish, Harvard University, Heinemann Asia, Maya Press, MPH, National University of Singapore, National Arts Council (Singapore), Pearson Education, Oxford University, Pearson–Longman, Penguin, Radio Fremantle, RNS Publications, Silverfish, Word Works and ZI.

Producers from Australia and New Zealand have offered to make movies of Shan's short stories. His work won the British Council Short Story Prize, came in second in the Oxford University Short Story Prize (judged by Iris Murdoch and John Bayley), received editor's choice in the Fish International Short Story Prize (Ireland) and won the Poetry Prize at Balliol College, Oxford University. He was published alongside three Nobel prizewinners, was first in his master's degree class at Harvard University with eight As and was on the Rhodes Scholarship Selectors Board. Shan has given many performance readings. He is now managing director at Trilogic after serving as general manager at Petronas and deputy secretary of the Treasury at the Ministry of Finance, Malaysia. *Marriage and Mutton Curry* is his first solo short-fiction collection.

ACKNOWLEDGEMENTS

HRH Sultan Nazrin Shah.

Epigram Books: Edmund Wee, Kenneth Wee, Jason Erik Lundberg, Lim Qin Yi.

Lat (Datuk Mohammad Nor Khalid).

Tony Crocker, Elaine Chiew, Ron Klein, Shirley Geok-Lin Lim, Sharon Bakar, Peter Carey, Tash Aw, Amir Muhammad, Mark O'Connor, Catherine Lim, Lim Soo Beng, Clem Cairns, Hugh Peyman, Dipika Mukherjee, Muhammad Haji Salleh, Hiroshi Matsuura, Robert Yeo, Ravi Chittampalli, Preeta Samarasan, Drummond Bone, Johan Jaaffar, Michael Vatikiotis.

Abhay Sardesai, Alfian Sa'at, Ameena Hussein, T. Ananda Krishnan, Ardashir Vakil, Baha Zain, Michael Backman, Ban Kah Choon, Marc Barety, Henry Barlow, Gail Billington, Cherie Blair, Richard Borsuk, Peter Hassan Brown, Sarah Butler, Chelva Kanaganayakam, Julian Candiah, Sabah Carrim, Margot Carrington, John Carruthers, Bernice Chauly, Chung Chee Min, Devena Kasinathan, Dina Zaman, Elliot Yahya Cohen, Barry Cole, Bob Cotton, Susila Cox, Mark Daniell,

John Dauth, Suzanne Davey, Nisha Dobberstein, Tutu Dutta, Ted Edmundson, Eric Forbes, Goh Heng Thean, Anthony Johae, Johari Razak, Marie Fernando, Lucy Friedland, VC George, Andrew Graham, Nelson Graves, Tunku Halim, Hew Chee Peng, Shirley Hew, Mary-Jane Holmes, Marie T. Hutalla, Louis James, Peter and Waveney Jenkins, Wolfgang Kasper, Ben Katchor, Kee Thuan Chye, Khaw Choon Ean, Khoo Kay Kim, Kirpal Singh, Shih-li Kow, Jacob Sam La-Rose, Aaron Lee, Daphne Lee, Lee Ee Leen, Francisca LePrince, Eva Lewin, Su-Chen Christine Lim, Richard Lord, Edwin Malachi, Kanagalingam Murugasu, K. S. Maniam, Mano Maniam, Mathilda Nathen, Ronnie and Susheila McCoy, Mirzan Mahathir, Simon Merrifield, Elizabeth Moggie, Daniel Mulhall, Robert Muscat, Navinan Rajeswaran, Ng Tieh Chuan, Nirgunan Tiruchelvam, Nizam Razak, Noraini Md. Yusof, Nor Faridah Manaf, Omar Merican, Ike Ong, Ooi Boon Leong, Alvin Pang, Patmalar Thuraisingham, Catherine Pippett, Nicholas Plant, K. Purushothaman, M. A. Quayum, R. Sudarshan, Rehman Rashid, Robert Raymer, Saraswathy Velupillai Murugasu, Shivani Sivagurunathan, Sothie Paul Duraisamy, Suleiman Manan, Sunita Jeyaindran, Raman Krishnan, Tristan Russell, Ruzy Hashim, A. Samad Said, Judy Shaik, Gwen Smith, Don Snodgrass, Tan Joo Lan, Tan Koon San, Ted Mahsun, Tina

Isaacs, June Tresise, Peter Varghese, W. Satchithananthan, Gaby Schneidereit, Bruce and Carl Sivalingam, Hugh Webb, Peter Wicks, John Wiggins, T. Wignesan, Alan Wong, Wong Ming Yook, Winnie Wong, Razali Wong Phui Nam, Margaret Yong.